LOST IN SPACE

'WARRIOR SMITH'

Written by
BRIAN McDONALD
Pencils by
GORDON PURCELL
Inks by
TERRY PALLOT & ANDE PARKS

Letters by
PAT BROSSEAU & CLEM ROBINS
Cover art by
GARY ERSKINE
Colors and Separations by
DIGITAL CHAMELEON

Publisher
MIKE RICHARDSON
Series Editors
PHILIP AMARA & IAN STUDE
Collection Editors
RACHEL PENN & IAN STUDE
Collection Designer
KRISTEN BURDA

DARK HORSE COMICS®

SPECIAL THANKS TO
DAVE IMHOFF AND HEIDI LIEBIG
AT NEW LINE CINEMA.

LOST IN SPACE™

THIS BOOK COLLECTS ISSUES 1 - 3 OF THE DARK
HORSE COMIC-BOOK SERIES LOST IN SPACE™.

FIRST EDITION: AUGUST 1998
ISBN: 1-56971-341-3

10 9 8 7 6 5 4 3 2 1
PRINTED IN CANADA

PUBLISHED BY
DARK HORSE COMICS, INC.
10956 SE MAIN STREET
MILWAUKIE, OR 97222

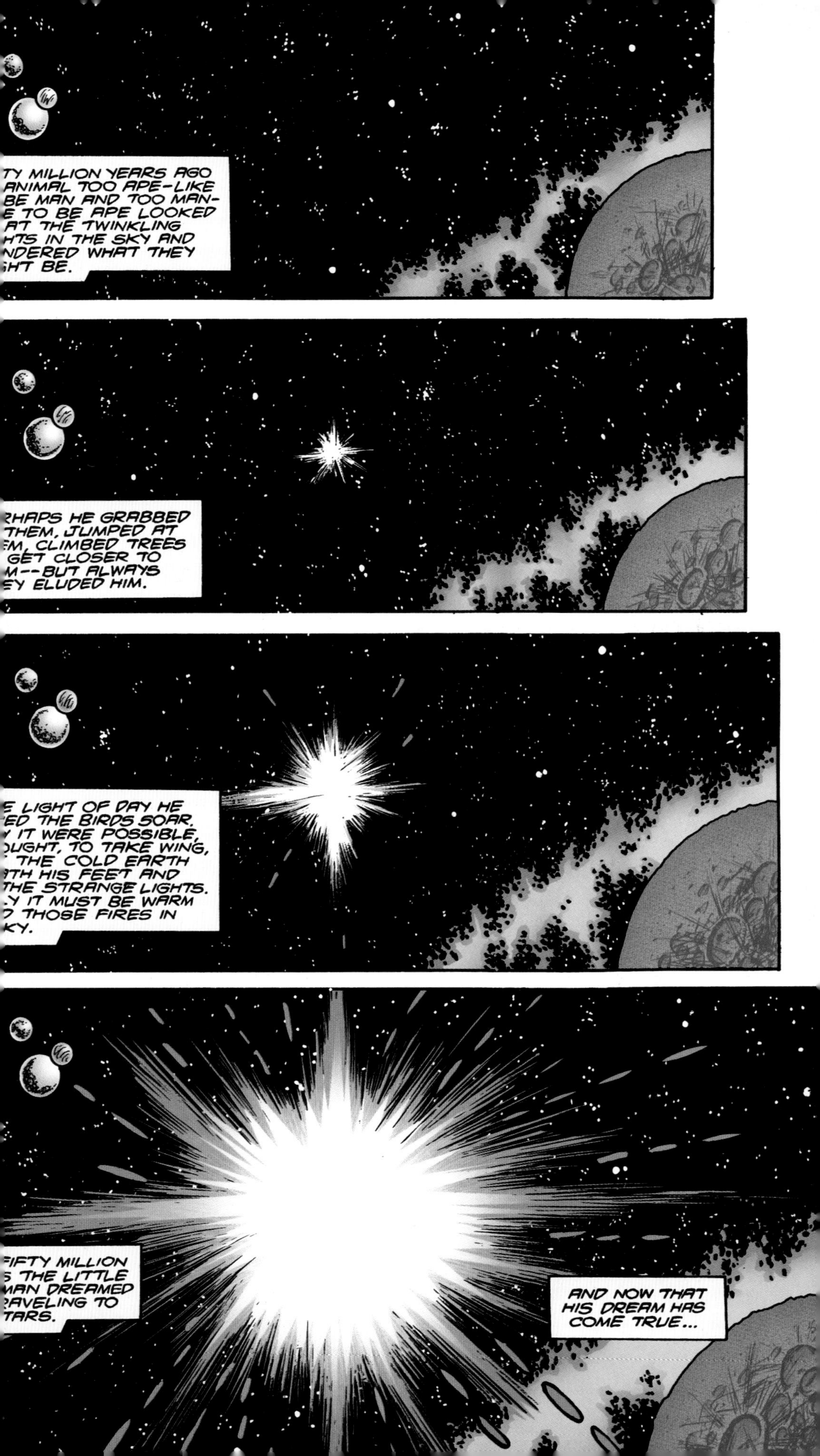

TY MILLION YEARS AGO ANIMAL TOO APE-LIKE BE MAN AND TOO MAN- E TO BE APE LOOKED AT THE TWINKLING HTS IN THE SKY AND NDERED WHAT THEY HT BE.
RHAPS HE GRABBED THEM, JUMPED AT EM, CLIMBED TREES GET CLOSER TO M--BUT ALWAYS EY ELUDED HIM.
E LIGHT OF DAY HE ED THE BIRDS SOAR. IT WERE POSSIBLE, OUGHT, TO TAKE WING, THE COLD EARTH TH HIS FEET AND THE STRANGE LIGHTS. Y IT MUST BE WARM THOSE FIRES IN KY.
FIFTY MILLION S THE LITTLE MAN DREAMED RAVELING TO TARS.
AND NOW THAT HIS DREAM HAS COME TRUE...

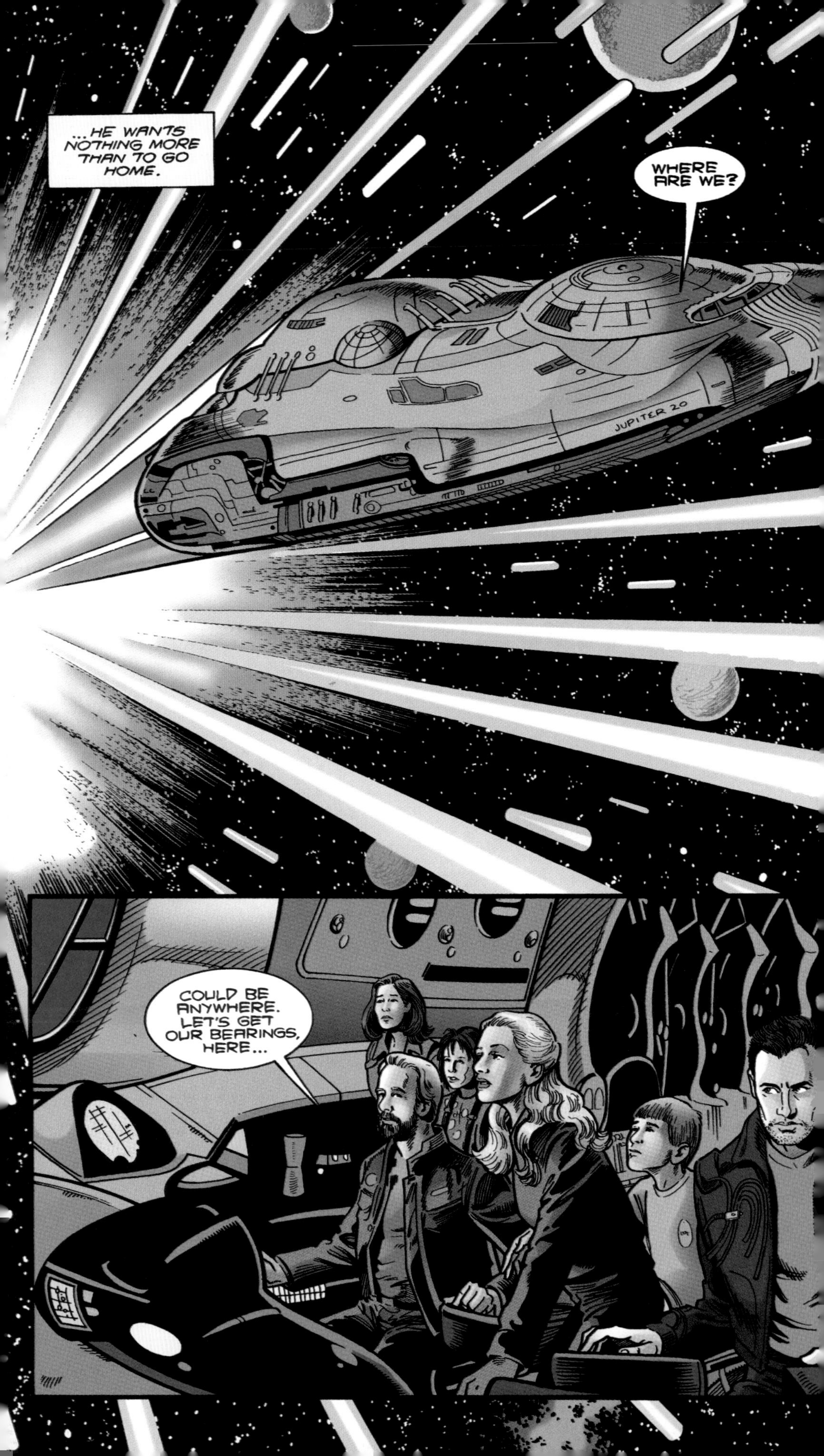
...HE WANTS NOTHING MORE THAN TO GO HOME.
WHERE ARE WE?
JUPITER 2
COULD BE ANYWHERE. LET'S GET OUR BEARINGS, HERE...

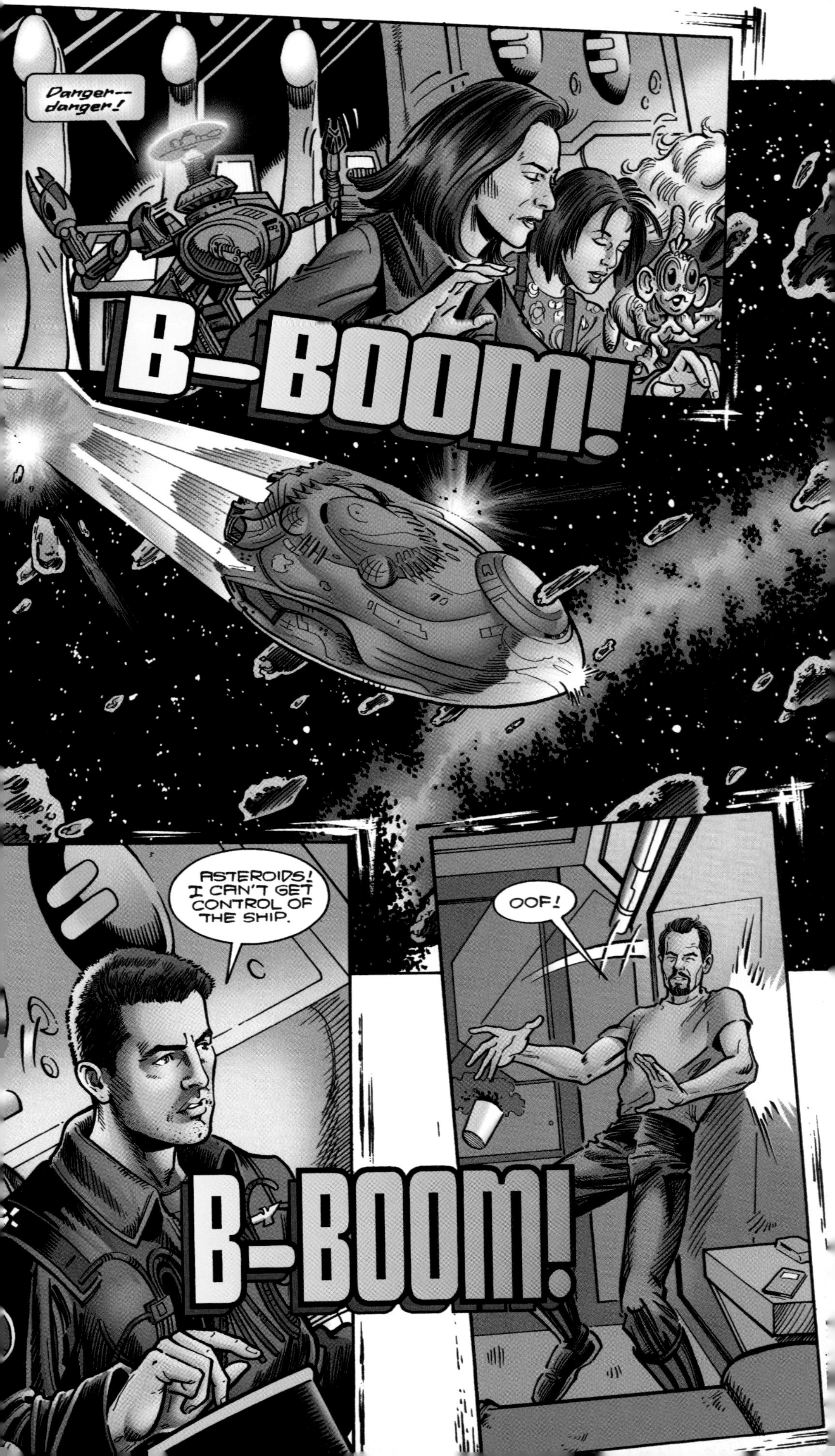
Danger--- danger!
B-BOOM!
ASTEROIDS! I CAN'T GET CONTROL OF THE SHIP.
OOF!
B-BOOM!

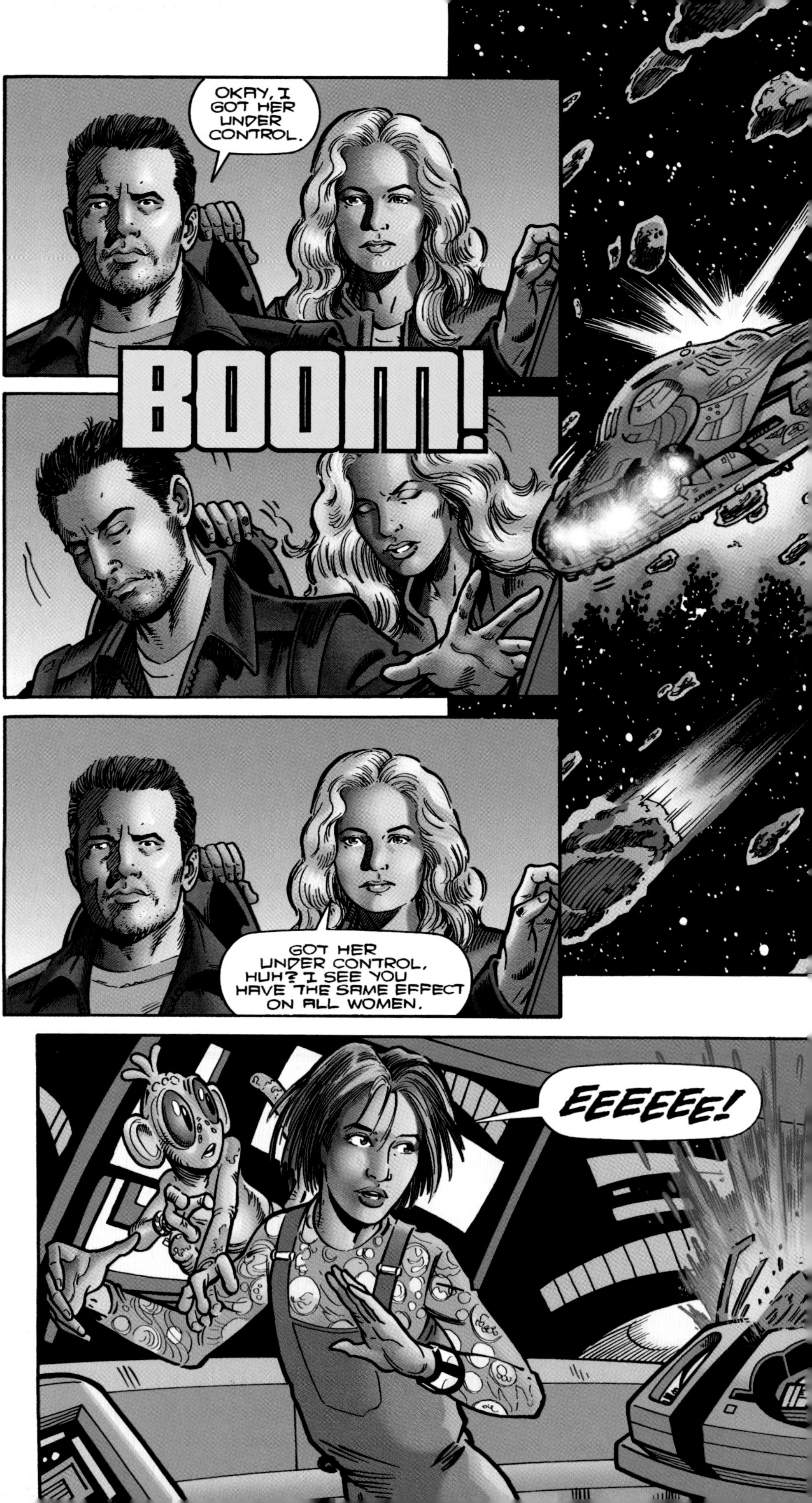
OKAY, I GOT HER UNDER CONTROL.
BOOM!
GOT HER UNDER CONTROL, HUH? I SEE YOU HAVE THE SAME EFFECT ON ALL WOMEN.
EEEEEE!

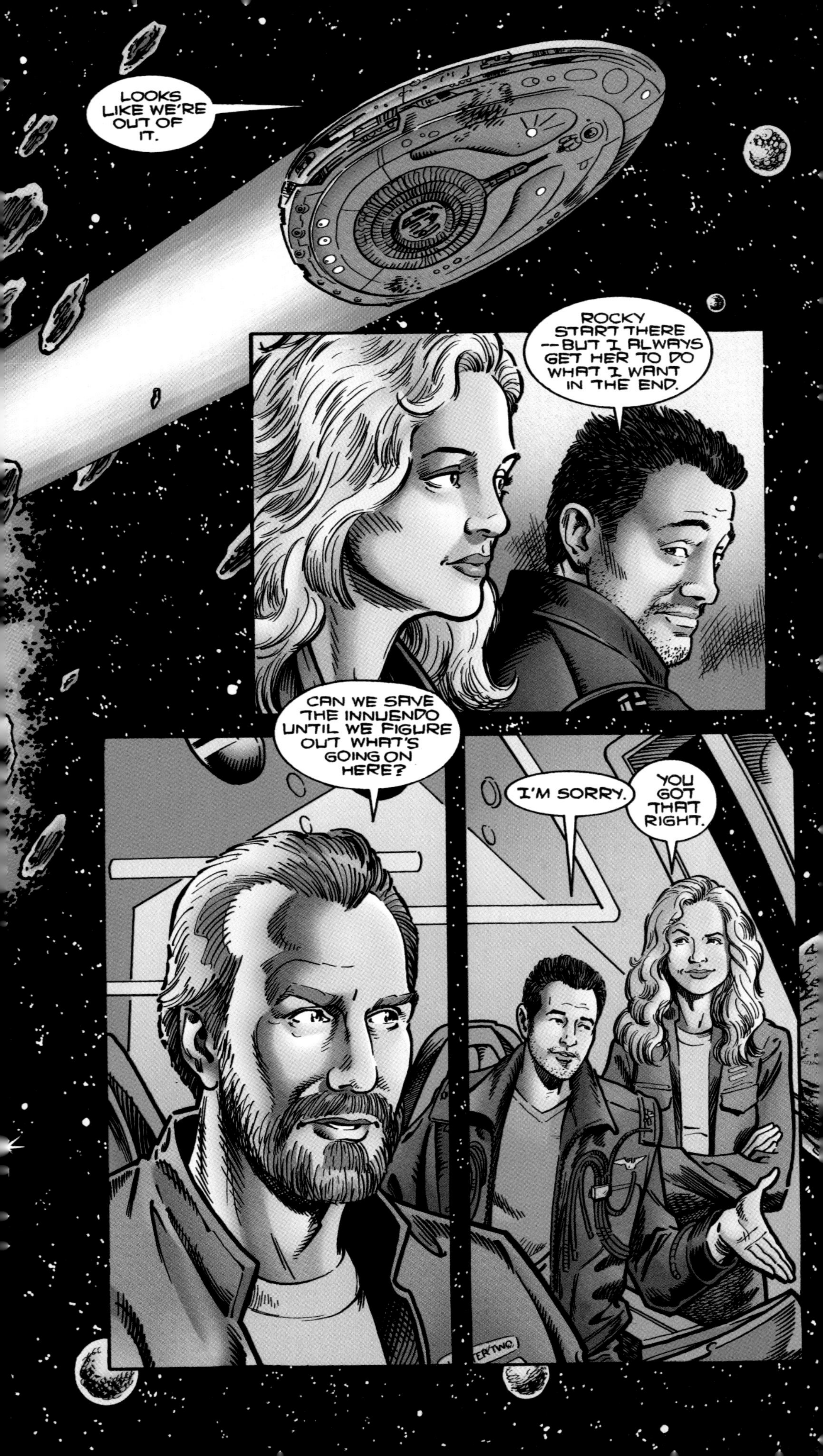
LOOKS LIKE WE'RE OUT OF IT.
ROCKY START THERE --BUT I ALWAYS GET HER TO DO WHAT I WANT IN THE END.
CAN WE SAVE THE INNUENDO UNTIL WE FIGURE OUT WHAT'S GOING ON HERE?
I'M SORRY.
YOU GOT THAT RIGHT.

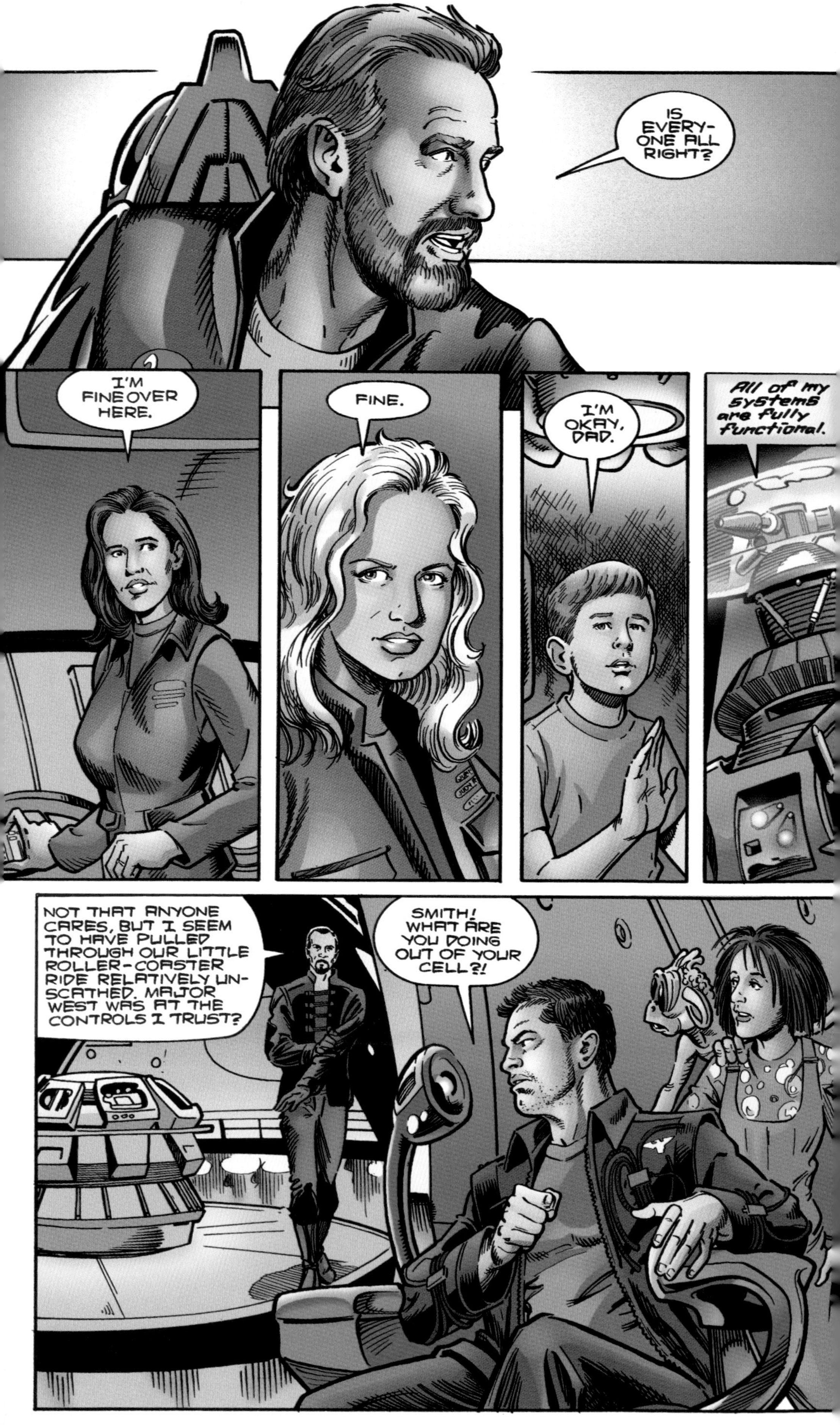
IS EVERY-ONE ALL RIGHT?
I'M FINE OVER HERE.
FINE.
I'M OKAY, DAD.
All of my systems are fully functional.
NOT THAT ANYONE CARES, BUT I SEEM TO HAVE PULLED THROUGH OUR LITTLE ROLLER-COASTER RIDE RELATIVELY UN-SCATHED. MAJOR WEST WAS AT THE CONTROLS I TRUST?
SMITH! WHAT ARE YOU DOING OUT OF YOUR CELL?!

ALL THAT BOUNCING AND BANGING AROUND CAUSED THE LOCKS TO MALFUNCTION.

HE'S RIGHT. ACTUALLY, A LOT OF THINGS WERE KNOCKED OFF LINE. UNLESS WE MAKE REPAIRS SOON WE COULD LOSE LIFE SUPPORT, GRAVITY, AND PROPULSION. THAT WAS QUITE A BIT OF DEBRIS WE HIT-- PROBABLY THE REMNANTS OF A PLANET.

TEK TEK-TEK BEEP

ACCORDING TO OUR SENSORS THERE'S A HABITABLE PLANET NOT FAR FROM HERE.

TEK-TEK BEEP

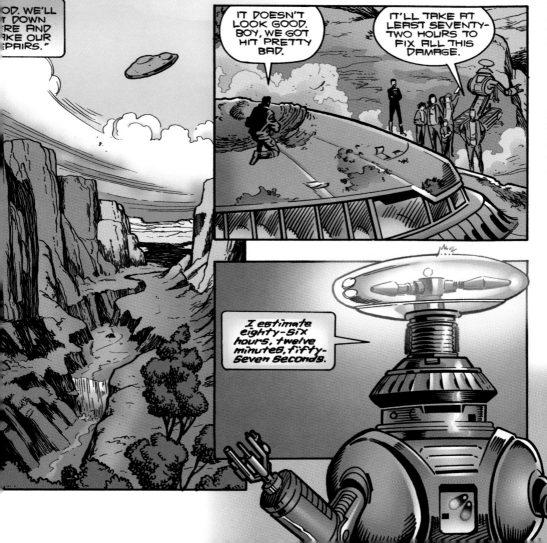

OD. WE'LL T DOWN RE AND KE OUR PAIRS."

IT DOESN'T LOOK GOOD. BOY, WE GOT HIT PRETTY BAD.

IT'LL TAKE AT LEAST SEVENTY-TWO HOURS TO FIX ALL THIS DAMAGE.

I estimate eighty-six hours, twelve minutes, fifty-seven seconds.

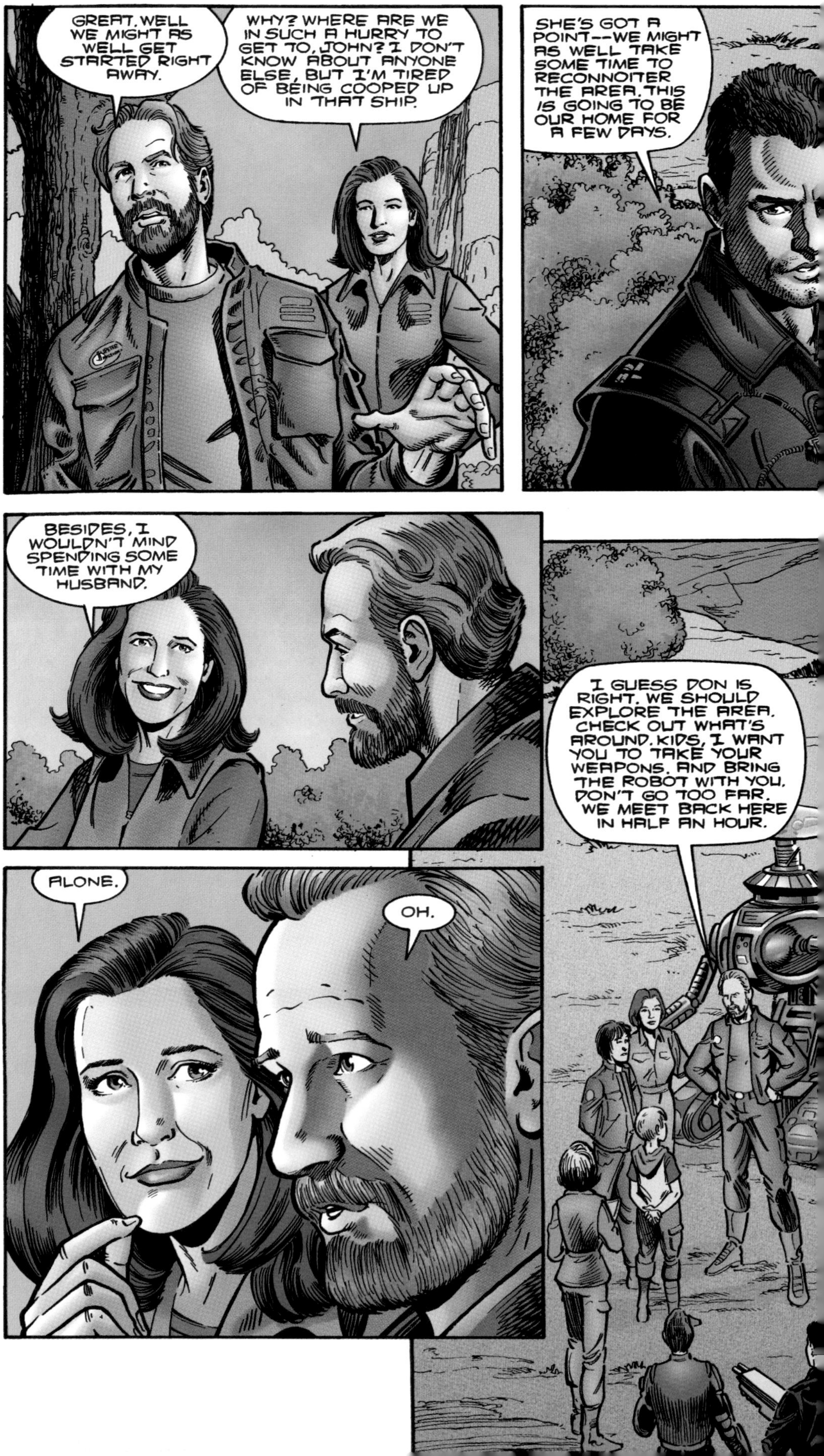
GREAT. WELL WE MIGHT AS WELL GET STARTED RIGHT AWAY.
WHY? WHERE ARE WE IN SUCH A HURRY TO GET TO, JOHN? I DON'T KNOW ABOUT ANYONE ELSE, BUT I'M TIRED OF BEING COOPED UP IN THAT SHIP.
SHE'S GOT A POINT--WE MIGHT AS WELL TAKE SOME TIME TO RECONNOITER THE AREA. THIS IS GOING TO BE OUR HOME FOR A FEW DAYS.
BESIDES, I WOULDN'T MIND SPENDING SOME TIME WITH MY HUSBAND.
ALONE.
OH.
I GUESS DON IS RIGHT. WE SHOULD EXPLORE THE AREA. CHECK OUT WHAT'S AROUND. KIDS, I WANT YOU TO TAKE YOUR WEAPONS. AND BRING THE ROBOT WITH YOU. DON'T GO TOO FAR. WE MEET BACK HERE IN HALF AN HOUR.

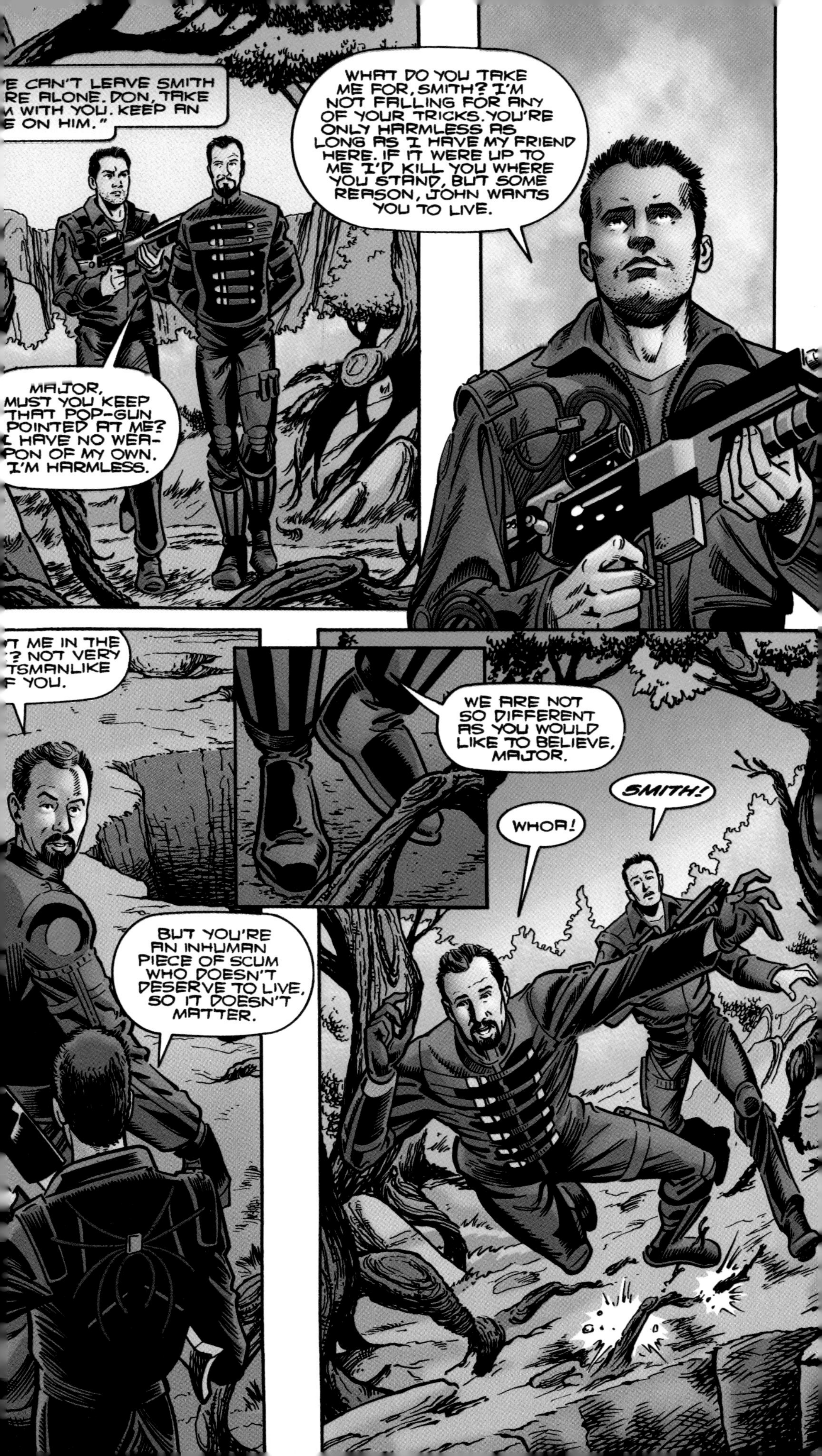

E CAN'T LEAVE SMITH RE ALONE. DON, TAKE M WITH YOU. KEEP AN E ON HIM."
MAJOR, MUST YOU KEEP THAT POP-GUN POINTED AT ME? I HAVE NO WEAPON OF MY OWN. I'M HARMLESS.
WHAT DO YOU TAKE ME FOR, SMITH? I'M NOT FALLING FOR ANY OF YOUR TRICKS. YOU'RE ONLY HARMLESS AS LONG AS I HAVE MY FRIEND HERE. IF IT WERE UP TO ME I'D KILL YOU WHERE YOU STAND, BUT SOME REASON, JOHN WANTS YOU TO LIVE.
T ME IN THE ? NOT VERY TSMANLIKE F YOU.
BUT YOU'RE AN INHUMAN PIECE OF SCUM WHO DOESN'T DESERVE TO LIVE, SO IT DOESN'T MATTER.
WE ARE NOT SO DIFFERENT AS YOU WOULD LIKE TO BELIEVE, MAJOR.
WHOA!
SMITH!

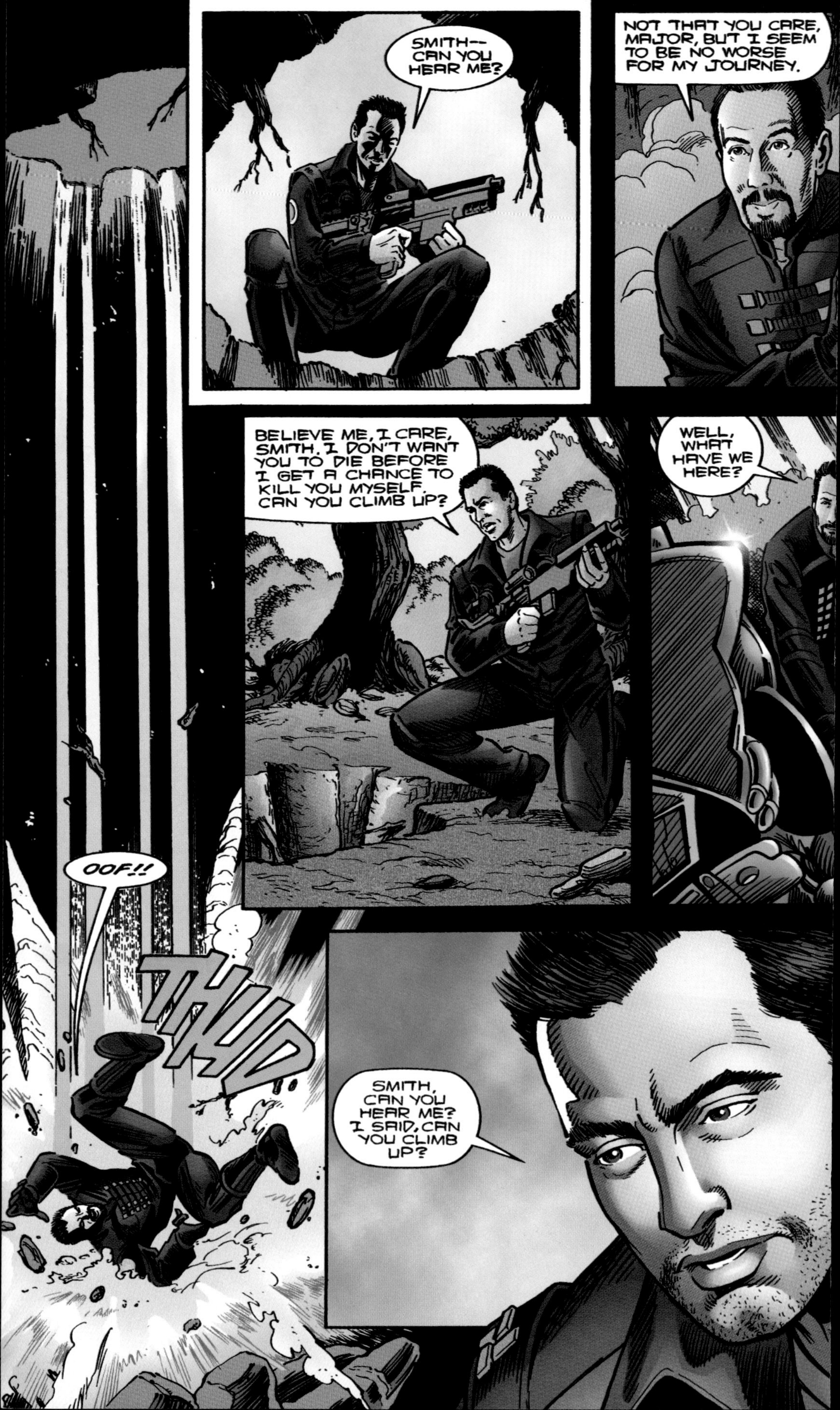
SMITH-- CAN YOU HEAR ME?
NOT THAT YOU CARE, MAJOR, BUT I SEEM TO BE NO WORSE FOR MY JOURNEY.
BELIEVE ME, I CARE, SMITH. I DON'T WANT YOU TO DIE BEFORE I GET A CHANCE TO KILL YOU MYSELF. CAN YOU CLIMB UP?
WELL, WHAT HAVE WE HERE?
OOF!!
THUD
SMITH, CAN YOU HEAR ME? I SAID, CAN YOU CLIMB UP?

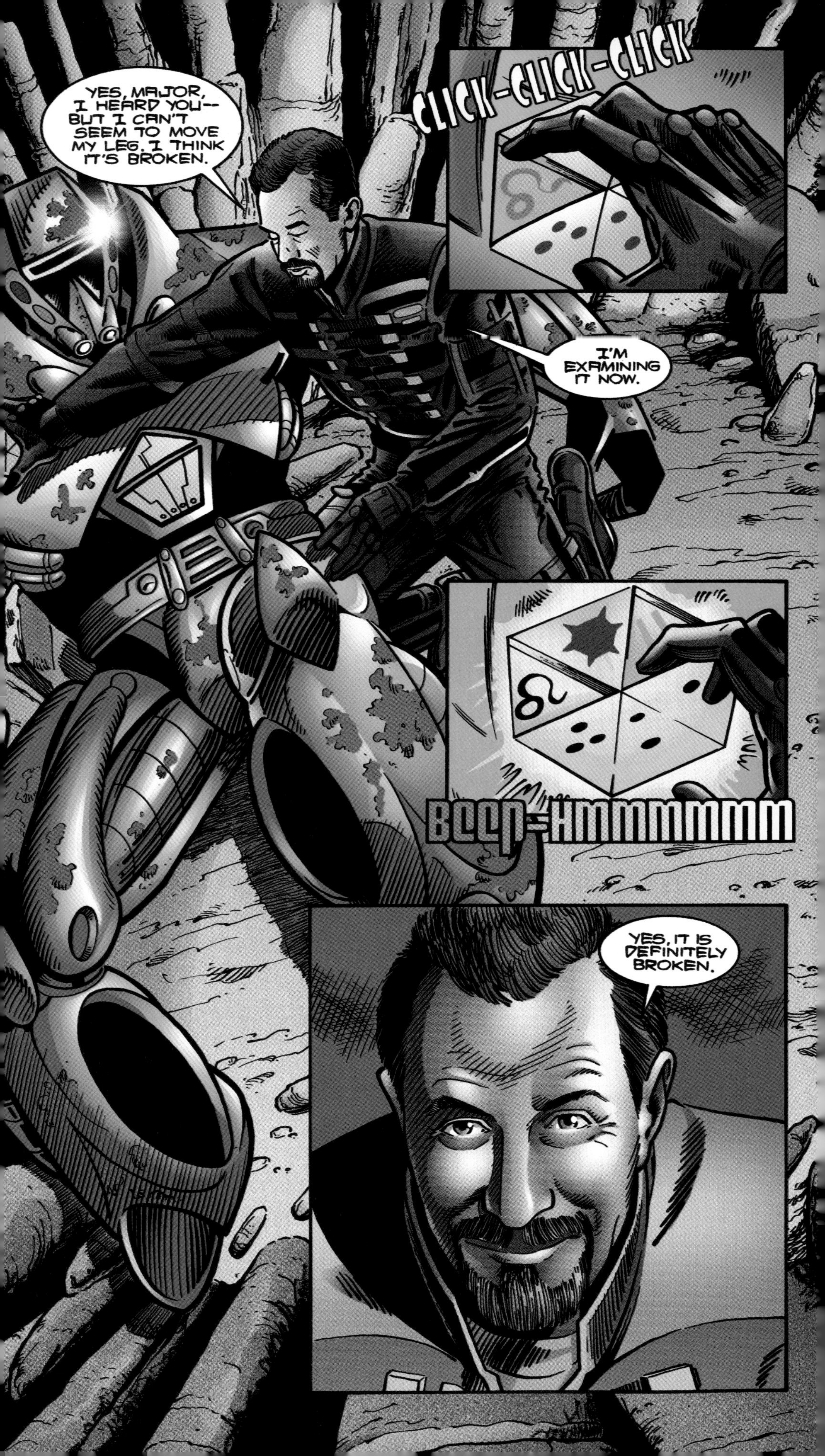
YES, MAJOR, I HEARD YOU-- BUT I CAN'T SEEM TO MOVE MY LEG. I THINK IT'S BROKEN.
CLICK-CLICK-CLICK
I'M EXAMINING IT NOW.
BEEP-HMMMMMMM
YES, IT IS DEFINITELY BROKEN.

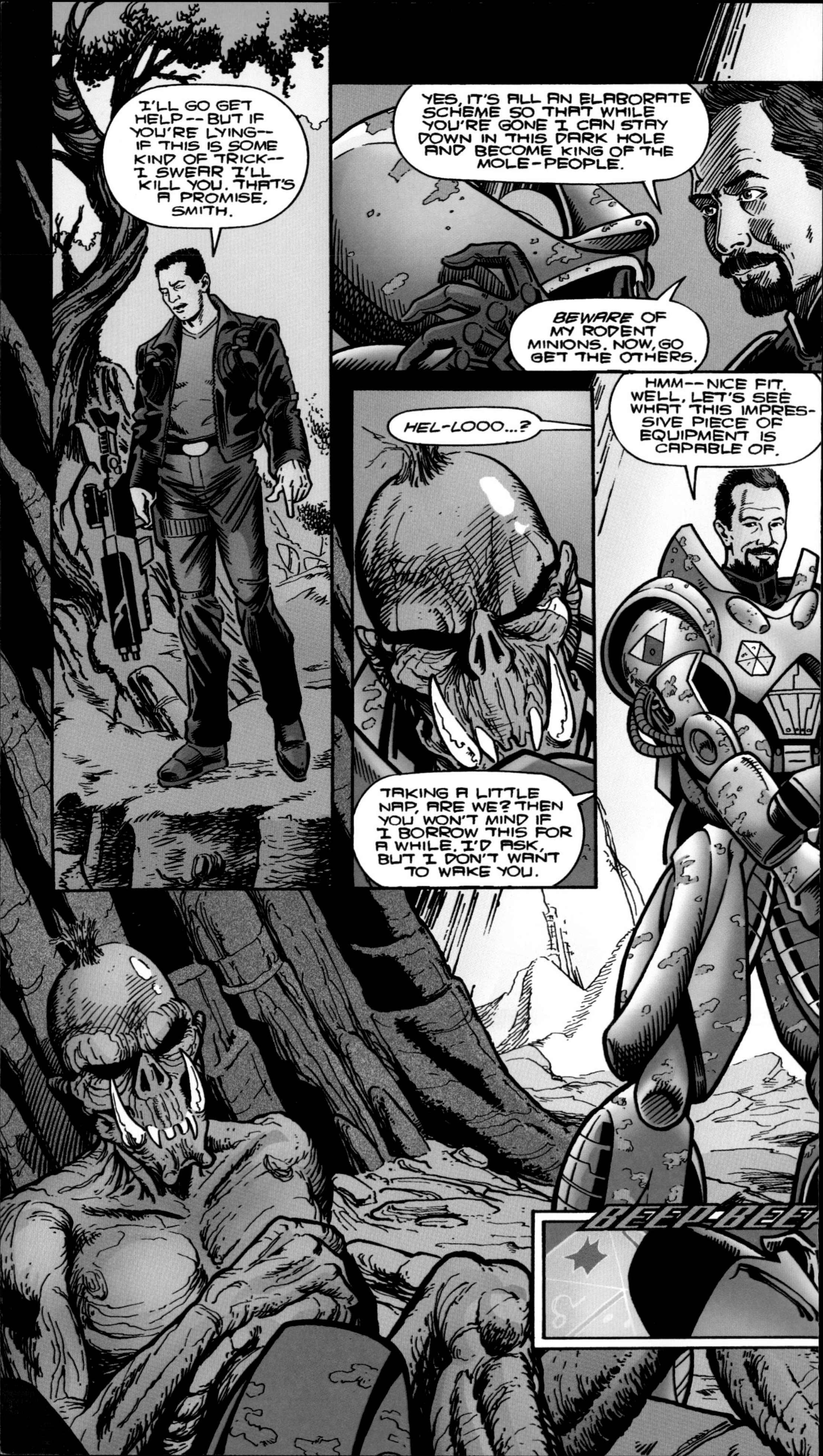
I'LL GO GET HELP--BUT IF YOU'RE LYING--IF THIS IS SOME KIND OF TRICK--I SWEAR I'LL KILL YOU. THAT'S A PROMISE, SMITH.
YES, IT'S ALL AN ELABORATE SCHEME SO THAT WHILE YOU'RE GONE I CAN STAY DOWN IN THIS DARK HOLE AND BECOME KING OF THE MOLE-PEOPLE.
BEWARE OF MY RODENT MINIONS. NOW, GO GET THE OTHERS.
HEL-LOOO...?
TAKING A LITTLE NAP, ARE WE? THEN YOU WON'T MIND IF I BORROW THIS FOR A WHILE. I'D ASK, BUT I DON'T WANT TO WAKE YOU.
HMM--NICE FIT. WELL, LET'S SEE WHAT THIS IMPRESSIVE PIECE OF EQUIPMENT IS CAPABLE OF.

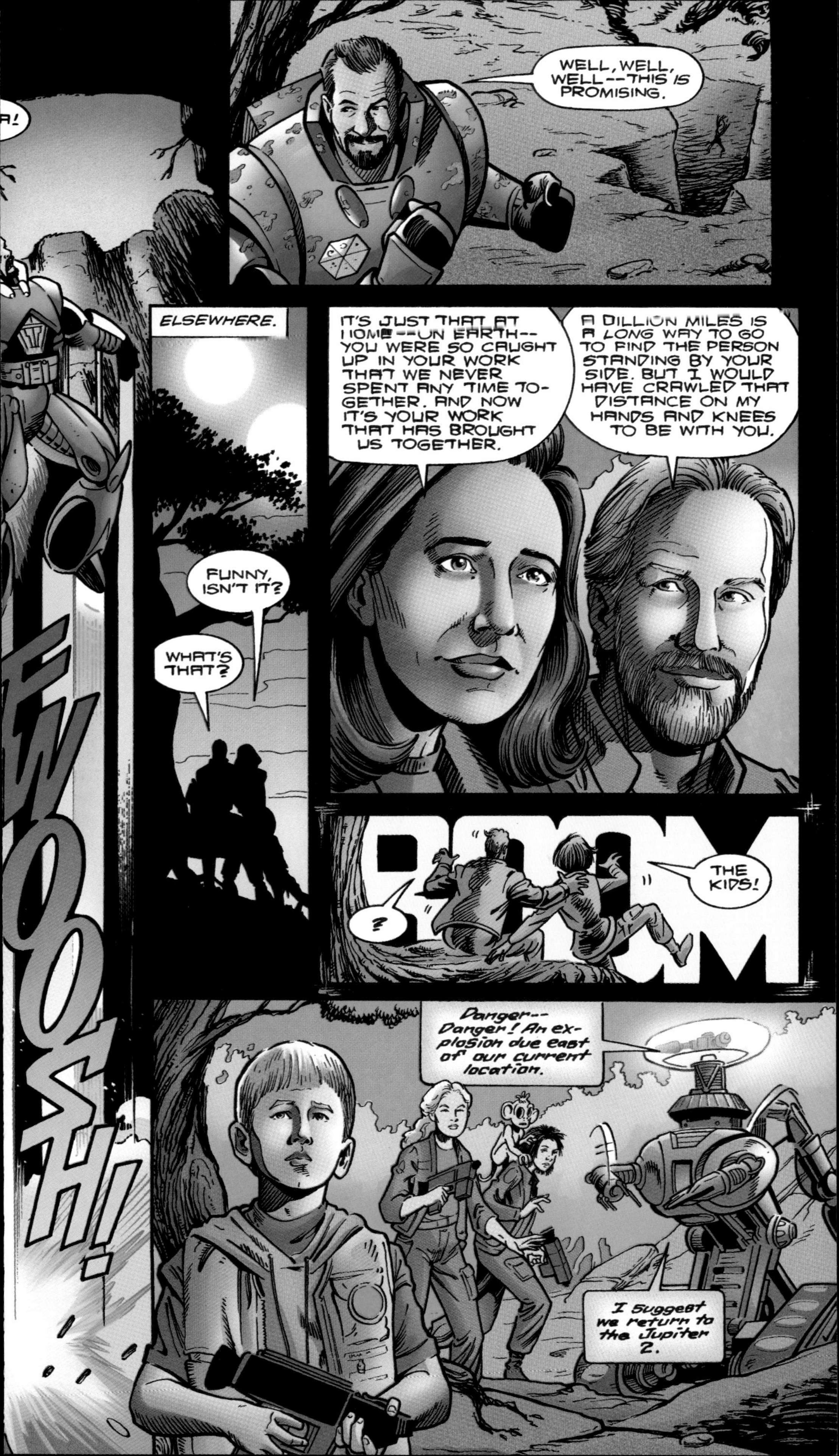

WELL, WELL, WELL--THIS IS PROMISING.
ELSEWHERE.
FUNNY, ISN'T IT?
WHAT'S THAT?
IT'S JUST THAT AT HOME--ON EARTH--YOU WERE SO CAUGHT UP IN YOUR WORK THAT WE NEVER SPENT ANY TIME TOGETHER. AND NOW IT'S YOUR WORK THAT HAS BROUGHT US TOGETHER.
A BILLION MILES IS A LONG WAY TO GO TO FIND THE PERSON STANDING BY YOUR SIDE. BUT I WOULD HAVE CRAWLED THAT DISTANCE ON MY HANDS AND KNEES TO BE WITH YOU.
BOOM
?
THE KIDS!
Danger--Danger! An explosion due east of our current location.
I suggest we return to the Jupiter 2.

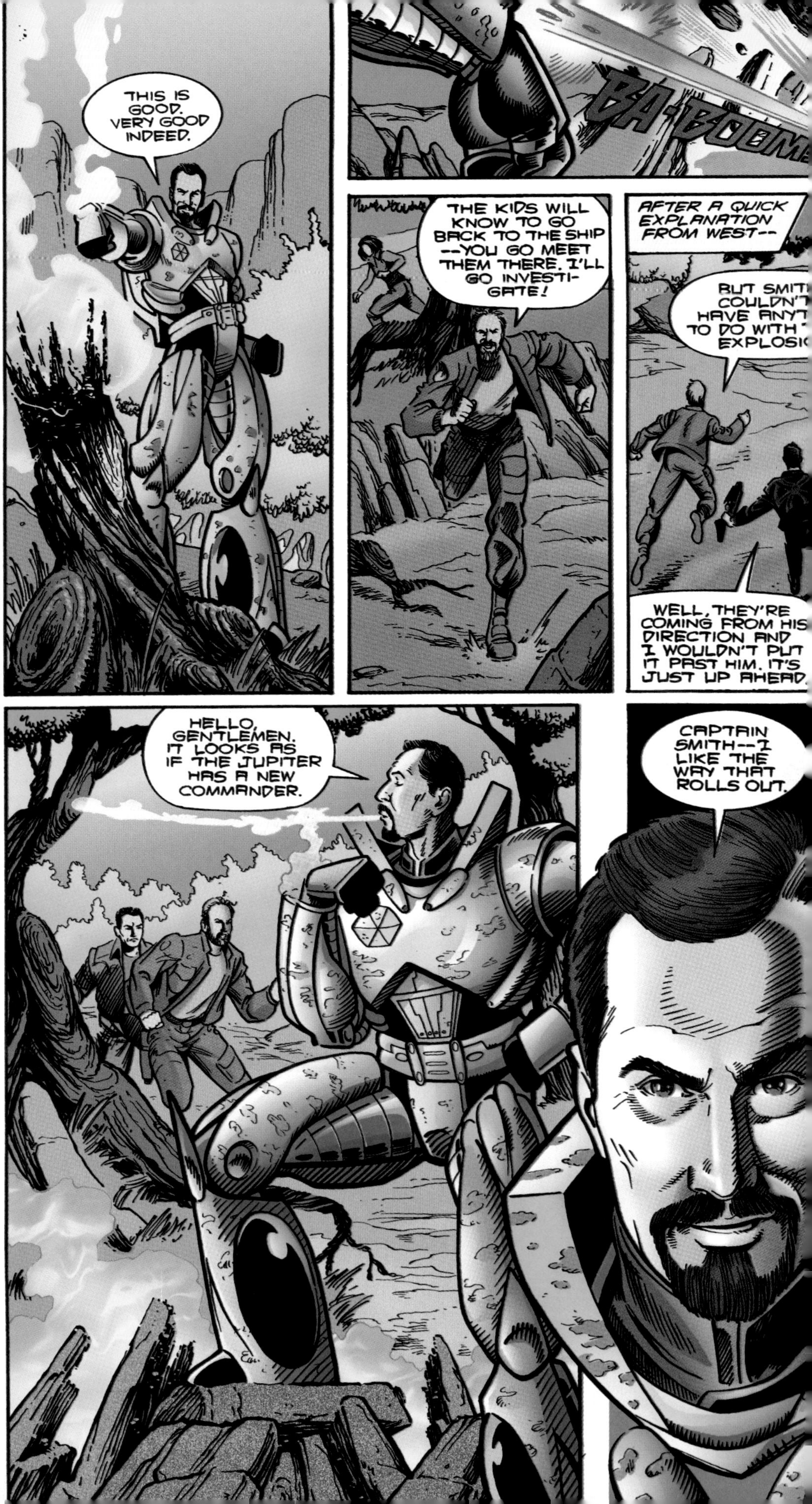

THIS IS GOOD. VERY GOOD INDEED.
BA-BOOM
THE KIDS WILL KNOW TO GO BACK TO THE SHIP --YOU GO MEET THEM THERE. I'LL GO INVESTIGATE!
AFTER A QUICK EXPLANATION FROM WEST--
WELL, THEY'RE COMING FROM HIS DIRECTION AND I WOULDN'T PUT IT PAST HIM. IT'S JUST UP AHEAD.
HELLO, GENTLEMEN. IT LOOKS AS IF THE JUPITER HAS A NEW COMMANDER.
CAPTAIN SMITH--I LIKE THE WAY THAT ROLLS OUT.

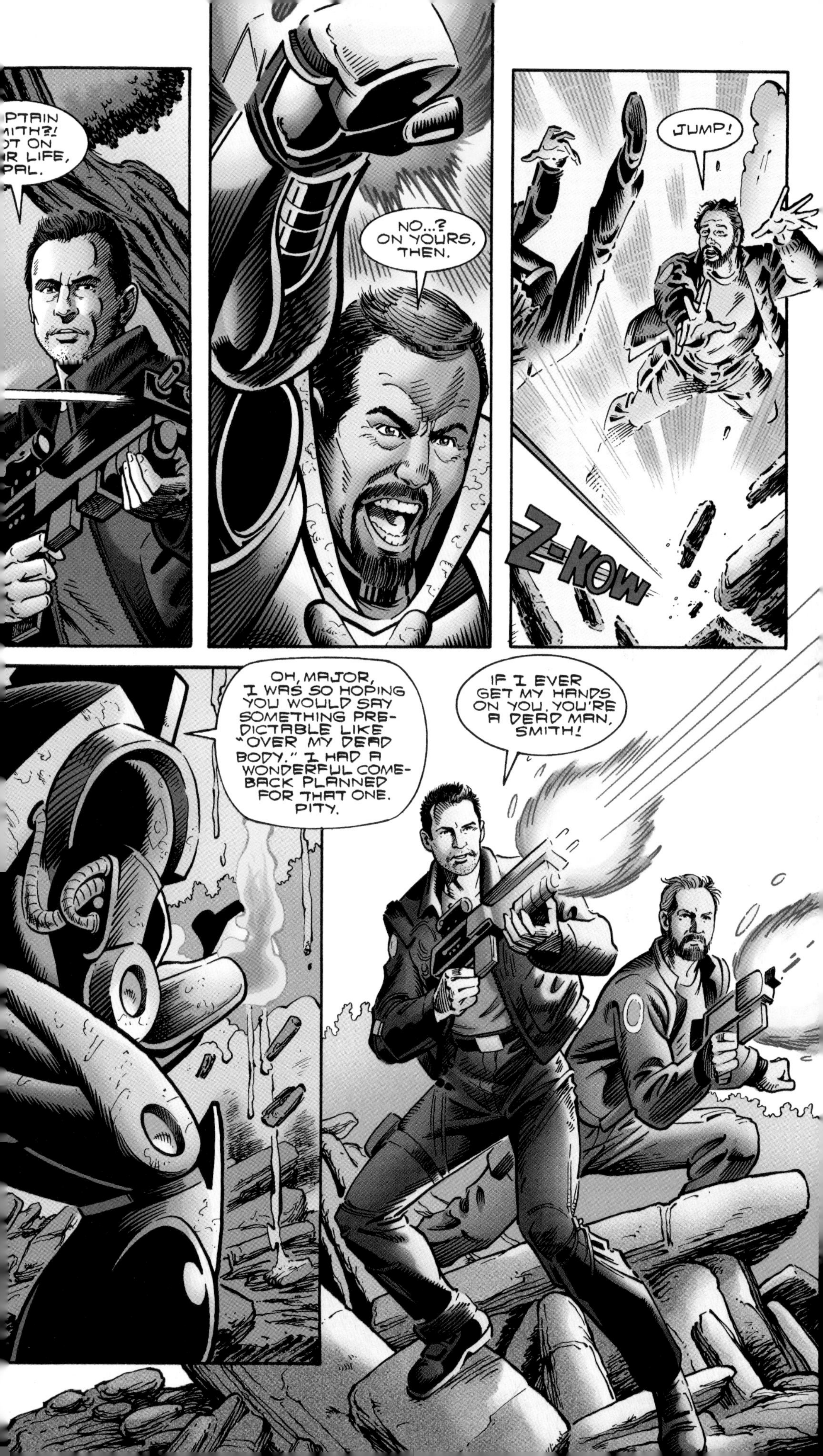
PTAIN
MITH?! OT ON
R LIFE,
PAL.
NO...? ON YOURS, THEN.
JUMP!
Z-KOW
OH, MAJOR, I WAS SO HOPING YOU WOULD SAY SOMETHING PRE-DICTABLE LIKE "OVER MY DEAD BODY." I HAD A WONDERFUL COME-BACK PLANNED FOR THAT ONE. PITY.
IF I EVER GET MY HANDS ON YOU, YOU'RE A DEAD MAN, SMITH!

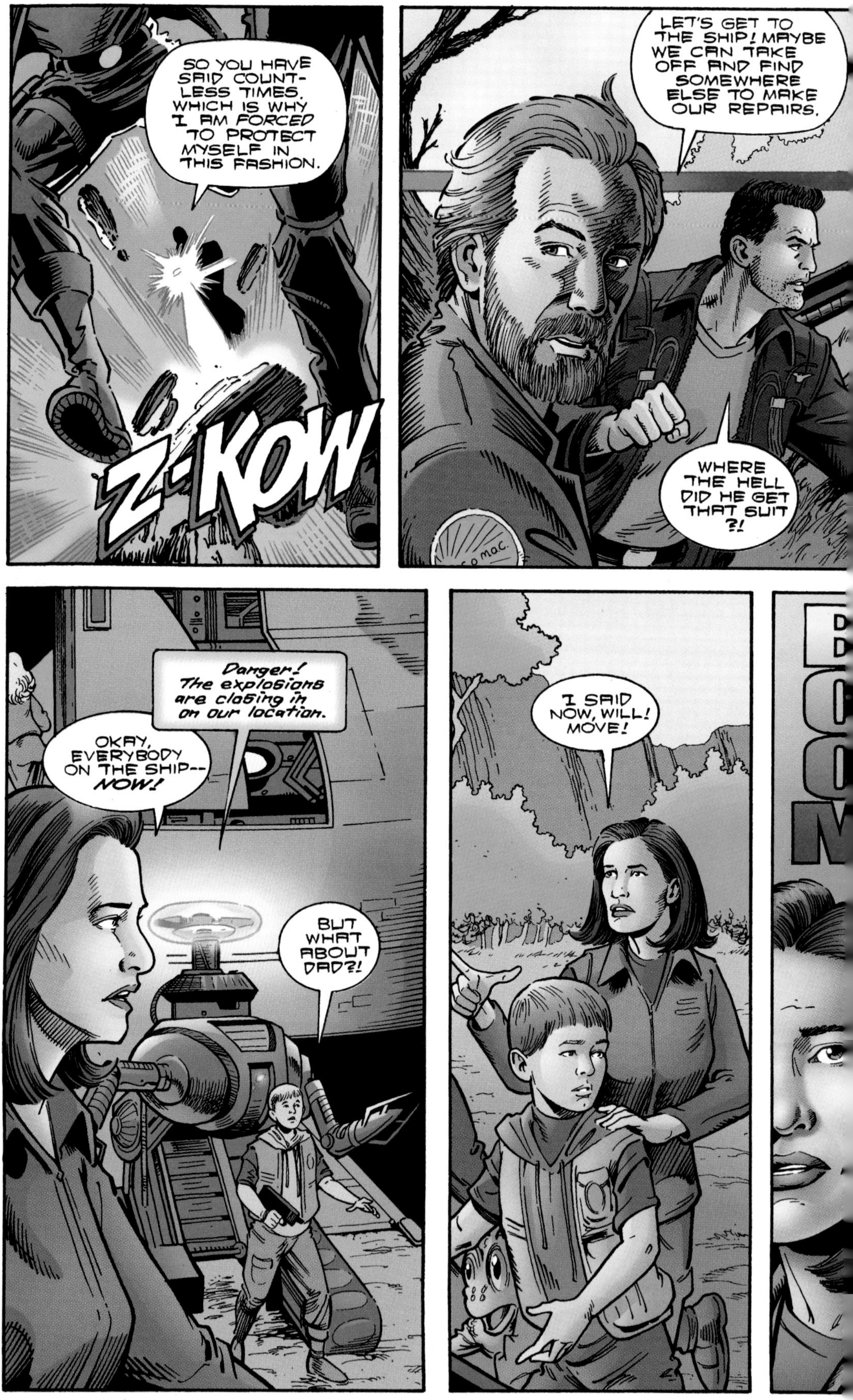

SO YOU HAVE SAID COUNT-LESS TIMES. WHICH IS WHY I AM FORCED TO PROTECT MYSELF IN THIS FASHION.
Z-KOW
LET'S GET TO THE SHIP! MAYBE WE CAN TAKE OFF AND FIND SOMEWHERE ELSE TO MAKE OUR REPAIRS.
WHERE THE HELL DID HE GET THAT SUIT ?!
OKAY, EVERYBODY ON THE SHIP-- NOW!
Danger! The explosions are closing in on our location.
BUT WHAT ABOUT DAD?!
I SAID NOW, WILL! MOVE!

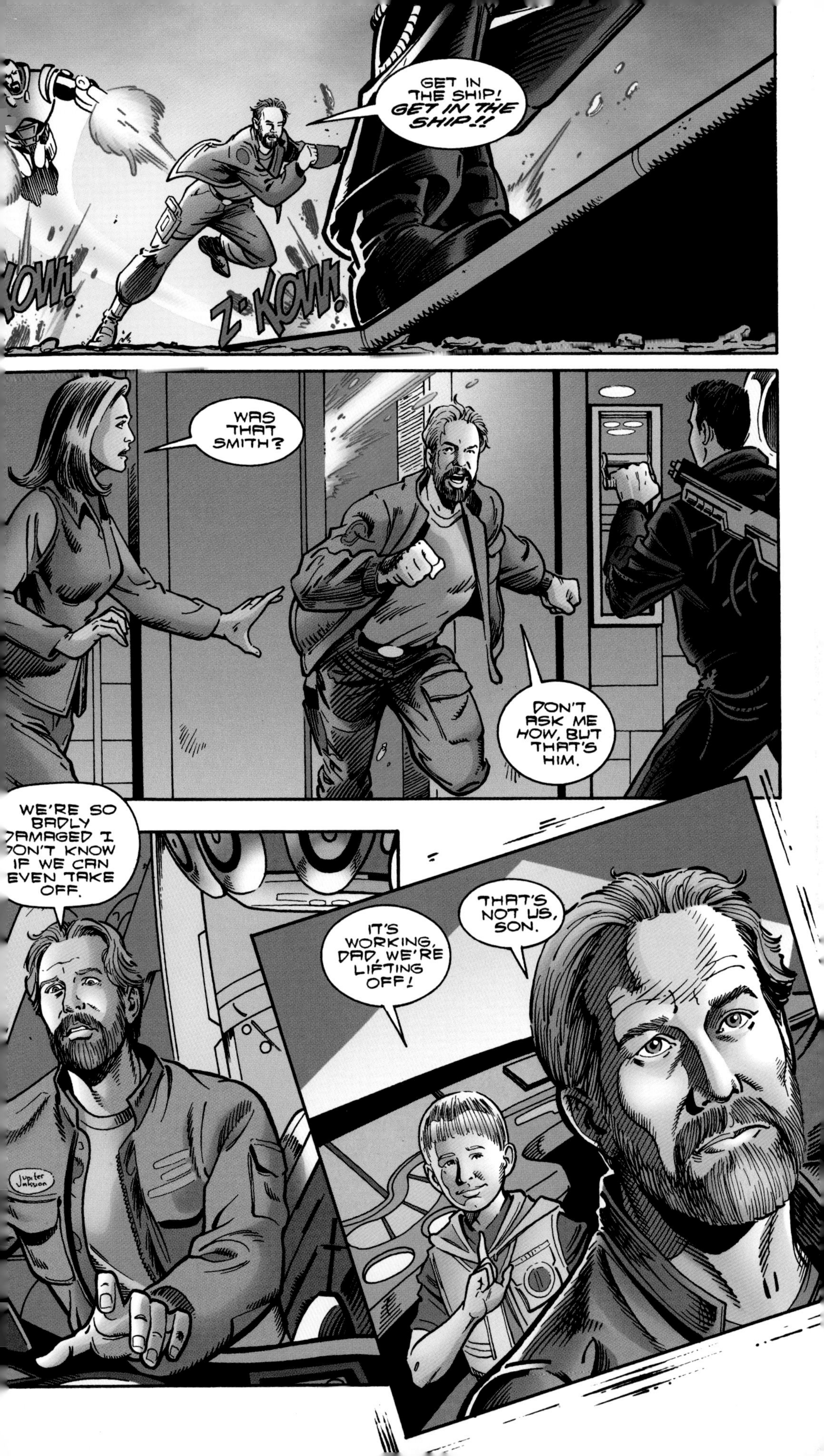
GET IN THE SHIP! GET IN THE SHIP!!
KOWW!
Z-KOWW!
WAS THAT SMITH?
DON'T ASK ME HOW, BUT THAT'S HIM.
WE'RE SO BADLY DAMAGED I DON'T KNOW IF WE CAN EVEN TAKE OFF.
IT'S WORKING, DAD, WE'RE LIFTING OFF!
THAT'S NOT US, SON.
Jupiter Jackson

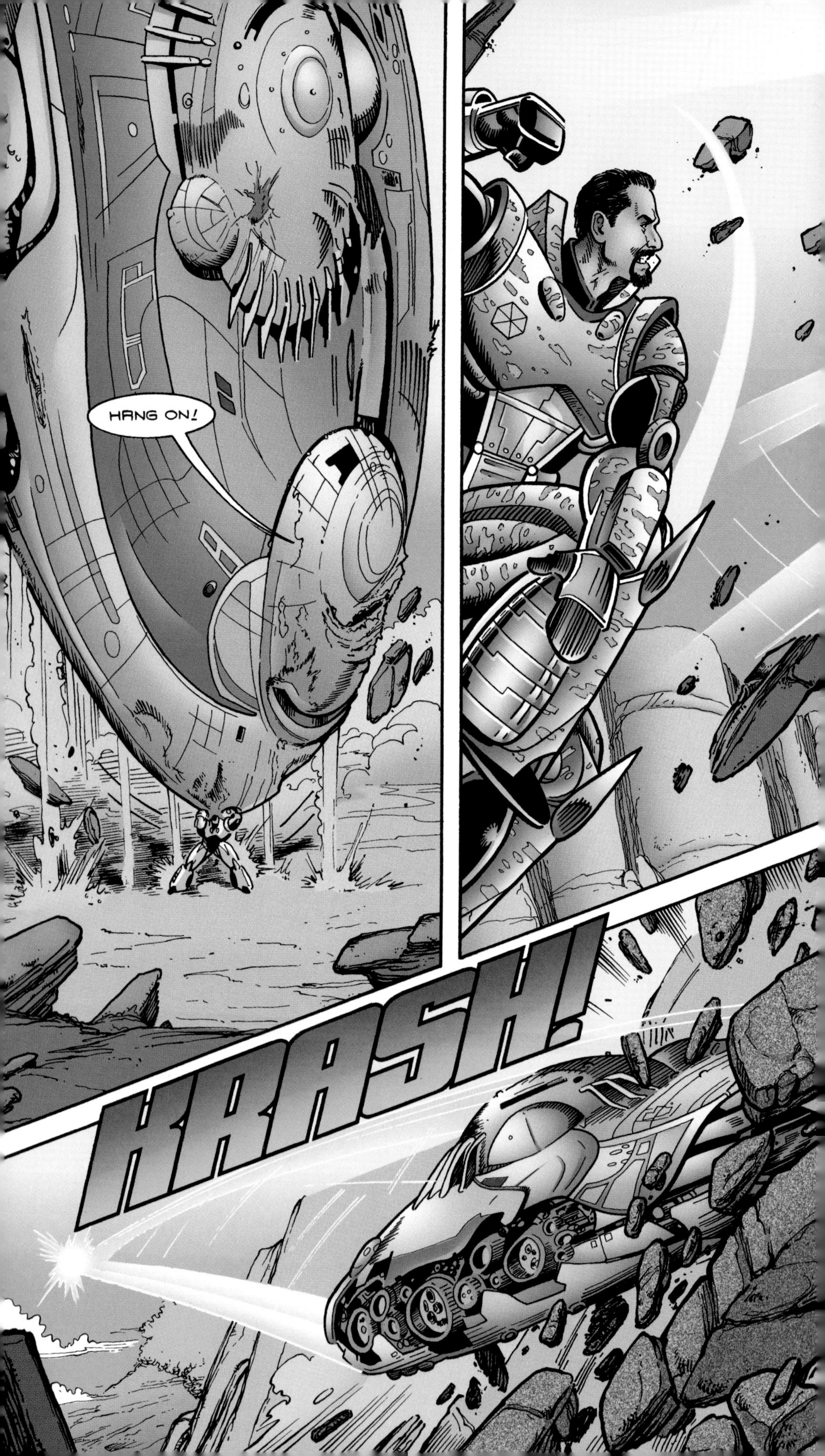
HANG ON!
KRASH!

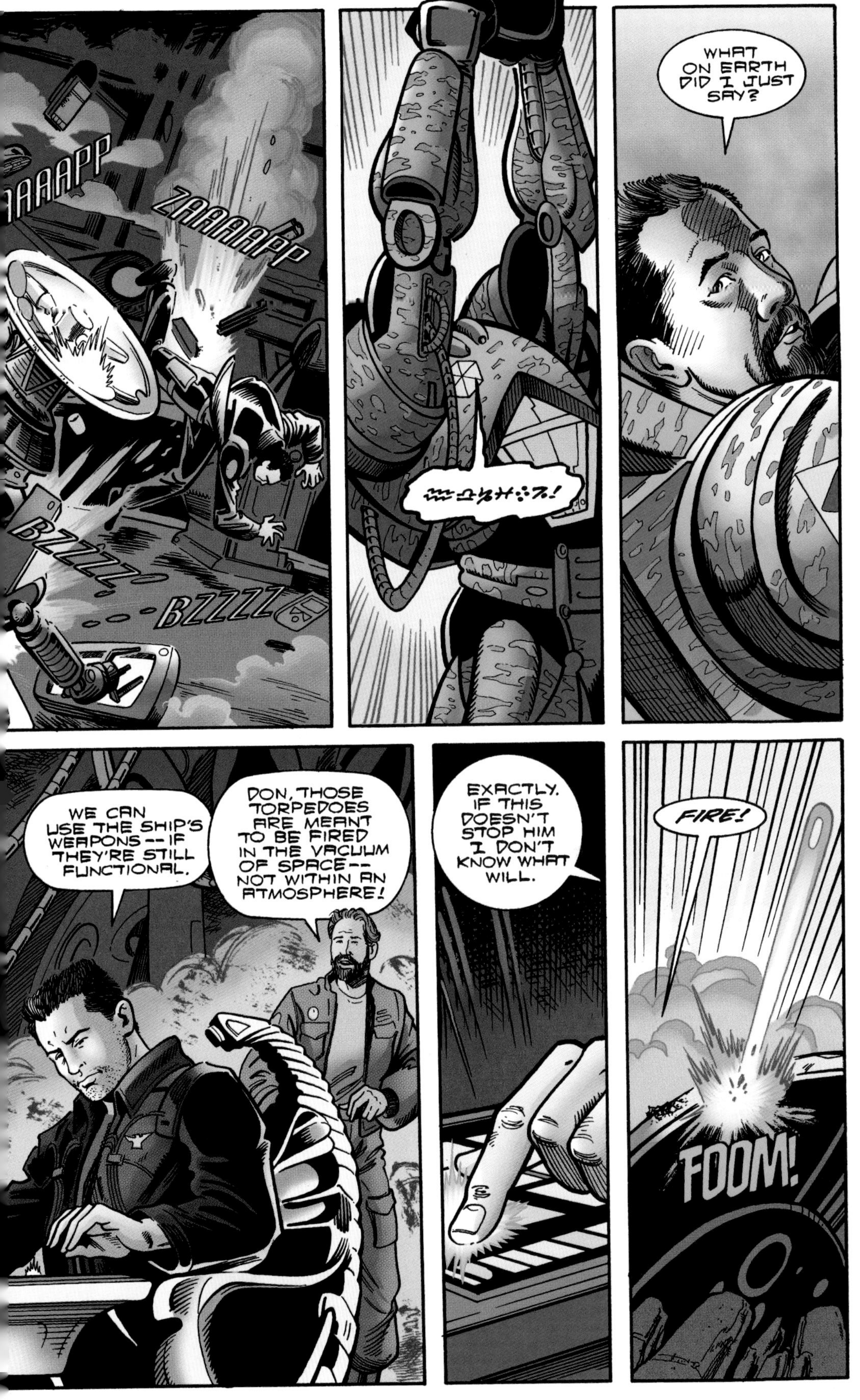
AAAAPP
ZAAAAAPP
BZZZZT
BZZZZ
WHAT ON EARTH DID I JUST SAY?
WE CAN USE THE SHIP'S WEAPONS -- IF THEY'RE STILL FUNCTIONAL.
DON, THOSE TORPEDOES ARE MEANT TO BE FIRED IN THE VACUUM OF SPACE -- NOT WITHIN AN ATMOSPHERE!
EXACTLY. IF THIS DOESN'T STOP HIM I DON'T KNOW WHAT WILL.
FIRE!
FOOM!

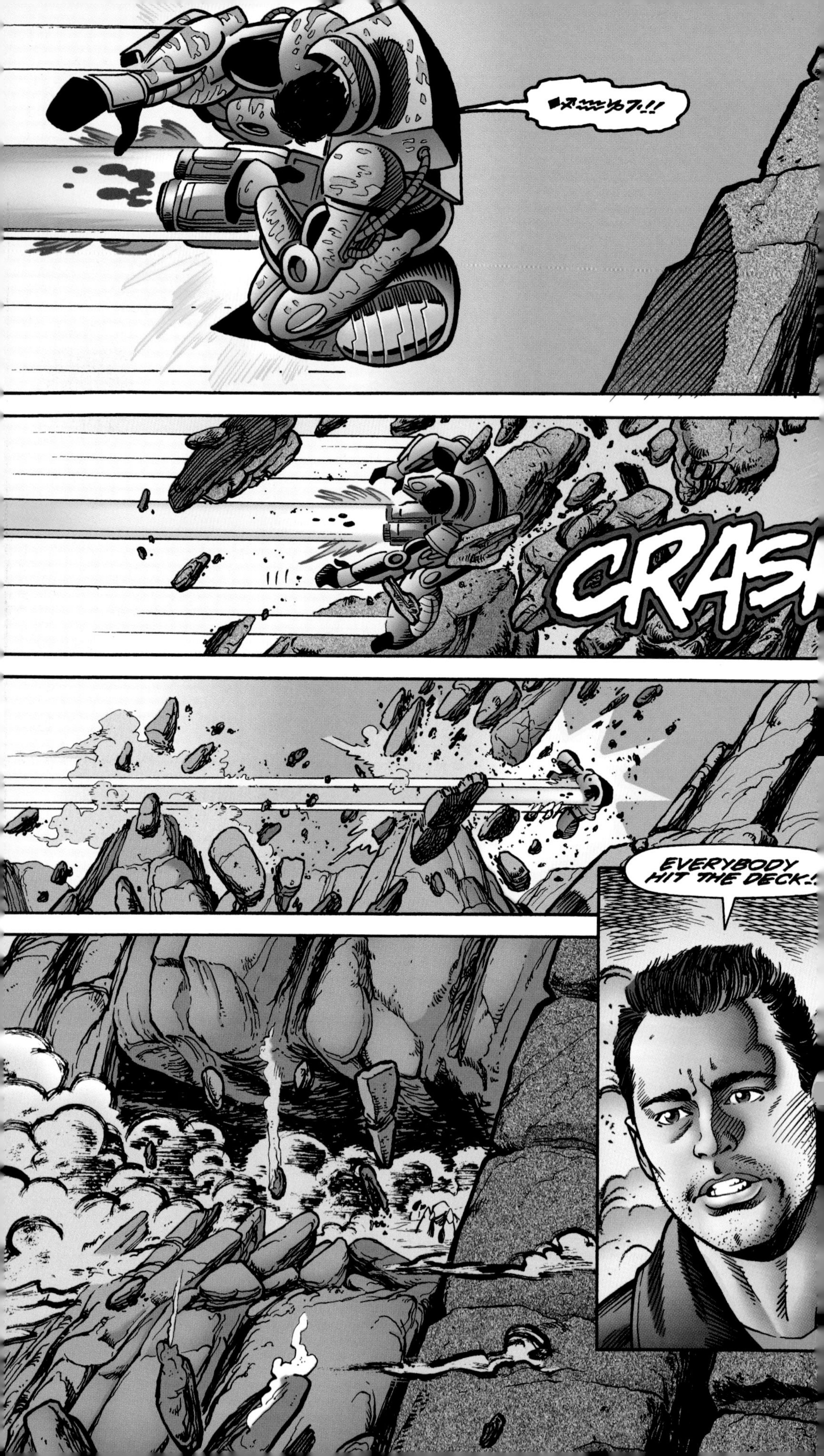
CRAS
EVERYBODY HIT THE DECK!!

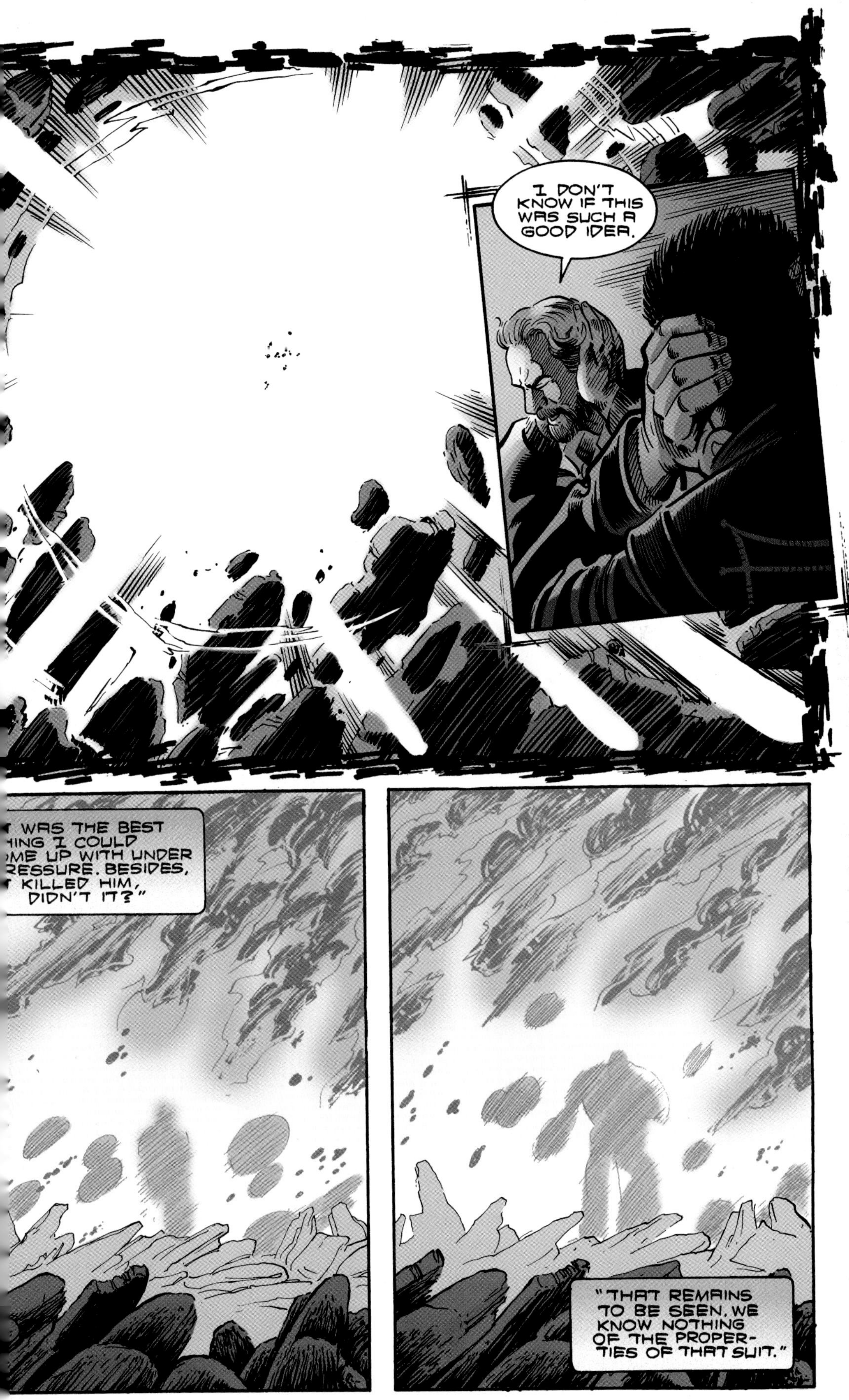
I DON'T KNOW IF THIS WAS SUCH A GOOD IDEA.
T WAS THE BEST HING I COULD OME UP WITH UNDER RESSURE. BESIDES, T KILLED HIM, DIDN'T IT?"
"THAT REMAINS TO BE SEEN. WE KNOW NOTHING OF THE PROPER-TIES OF THAT SUIT."

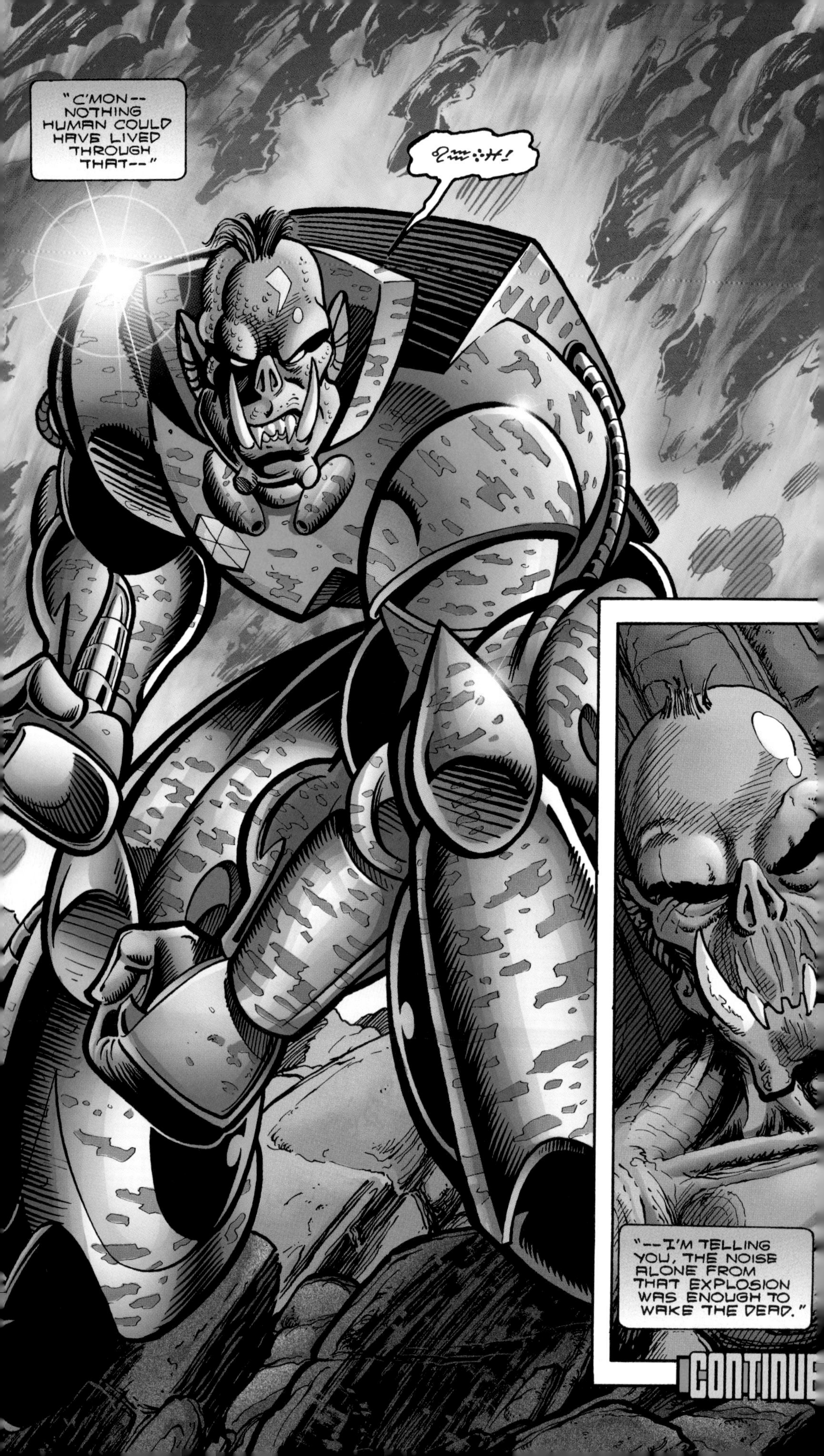
"C'MON--
NOTHING
HUMAN COULD
HAVE LIVED
THROUGH
THAT--"
"--I'M TELLING
YOU, THE NOISE
ALONE FROM
THAT EXPLOSION
WAS ENOUGH TO
WAKE THE DEAD."
CONTINUE

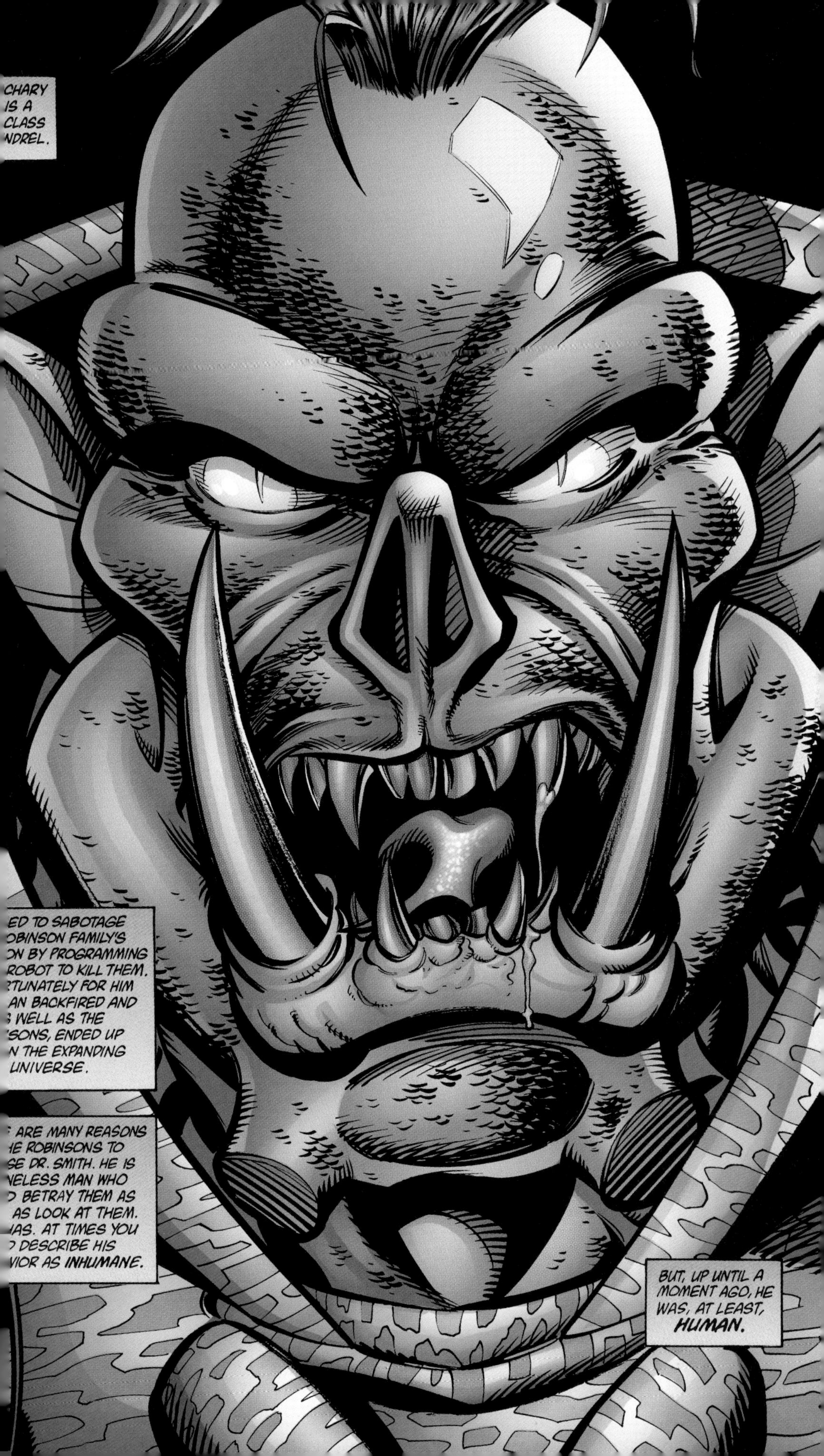
CHARY IS A CLASS NDREL.
ED TO SABOTAGE OBINSON FAMILY'S ON BY PROGRAMMING ROBOT TO KILL THEM. RTUNATELY FOR HIM AN BACKFIRED AND WELL AS THE SONS, ENDED UP N THE EXPANDING UNIVERSE.
ARE MANY REASONS HE ROBINSONS TO SE DR. SMITH. HE IS NELESS MAN WHO BETRAY THEM AS AS LOOK AT THEM. WAS. AT TIMES YOU DESCRIBE HIS VIOR AS INHUMANE.
BUT, UP UNTIL A MOMENT AGO, HE WAS, AT LEAST, HUMAN.

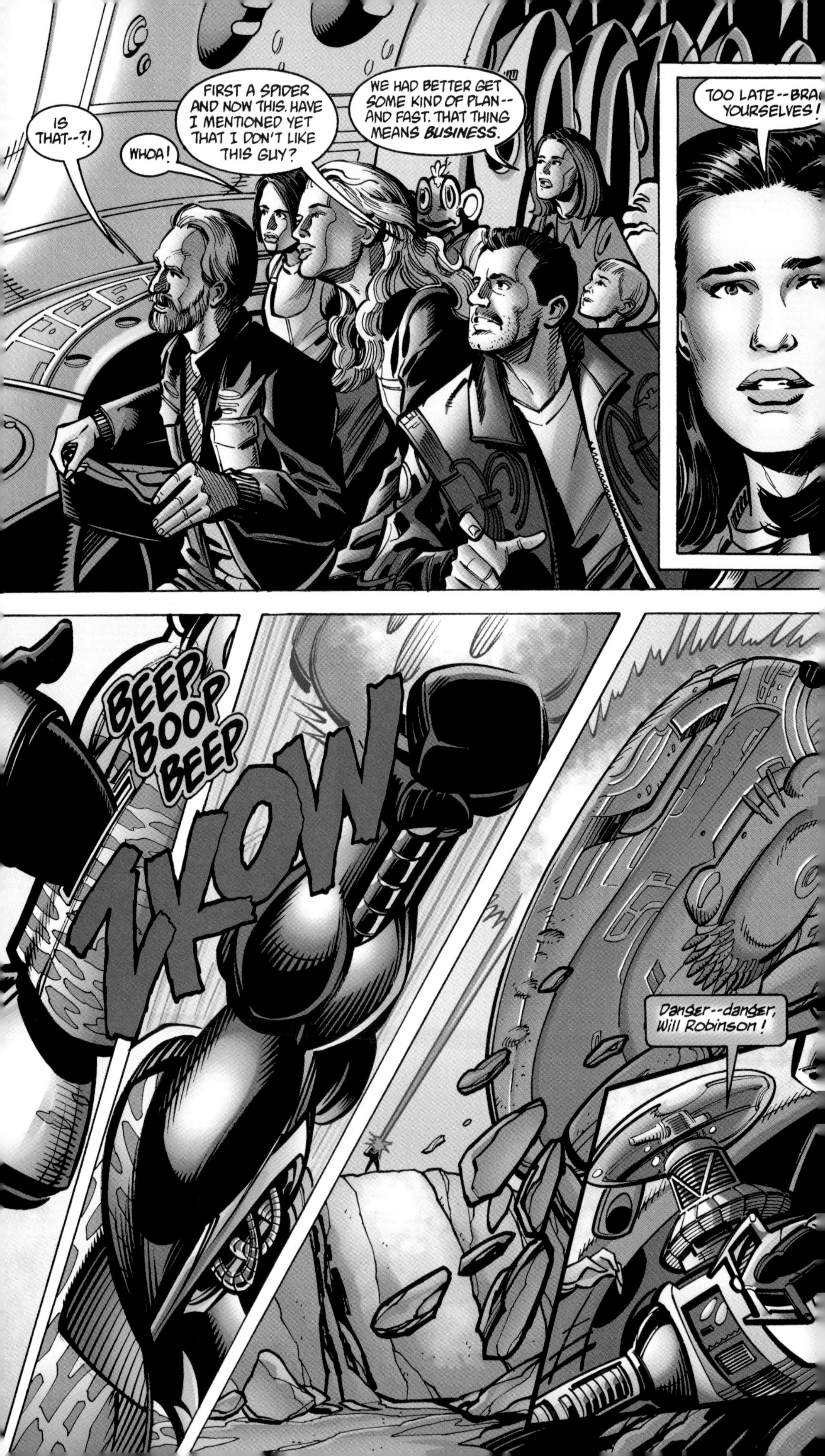
IS THAT--?!
WHOA!
FIRST A SPIDER AND NOW THIS. HAVE I MENTIONED YET THAT I DON'T LIKE THIS GUY?
WE HAD BETTER GET SOME KIND OF PLAN-- AND FAST. THAT THING MEANS BUSINESS.
TOO LATE--BRA YOURSELVES!
BEEP BOOP BEEP
KKOW
Danger--danger, Will Robinson!

EVERYBODY OKAY?

WE'RE FINE. TRY HITTING HIM WITH THE BLASTERS. IT WON'T STOP HIM, BUT MAYBE IT'LL SLOW HIM DOWN UNTIL WE THINK OF SOMETHING.

WAY AHEAD OF YOU. JUST AS SOON AS HE GETS A LITTLE CLOSER...

TEK BEEP

FIRE!

CHOOM

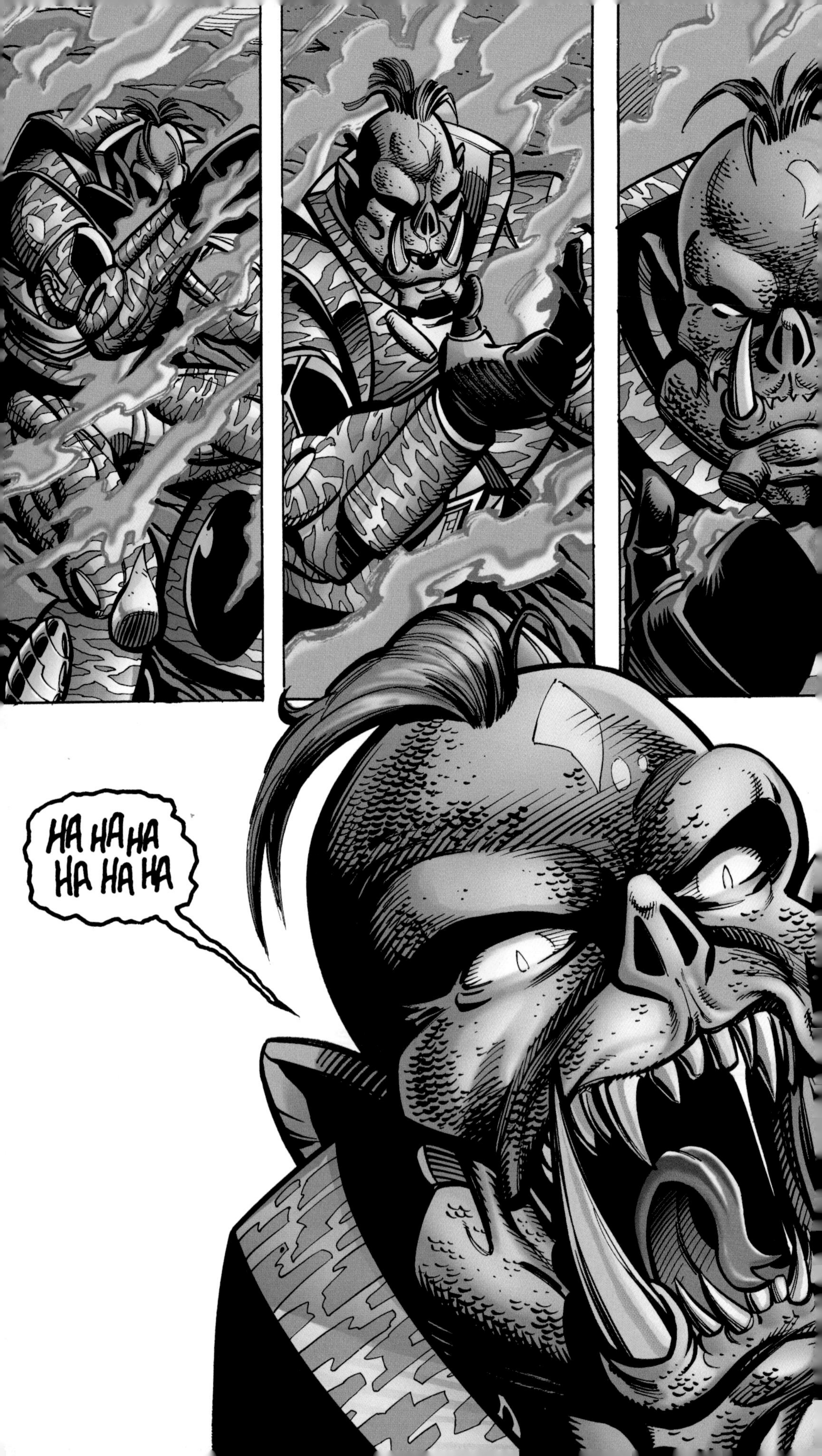
HA HA HA
HA HA HA

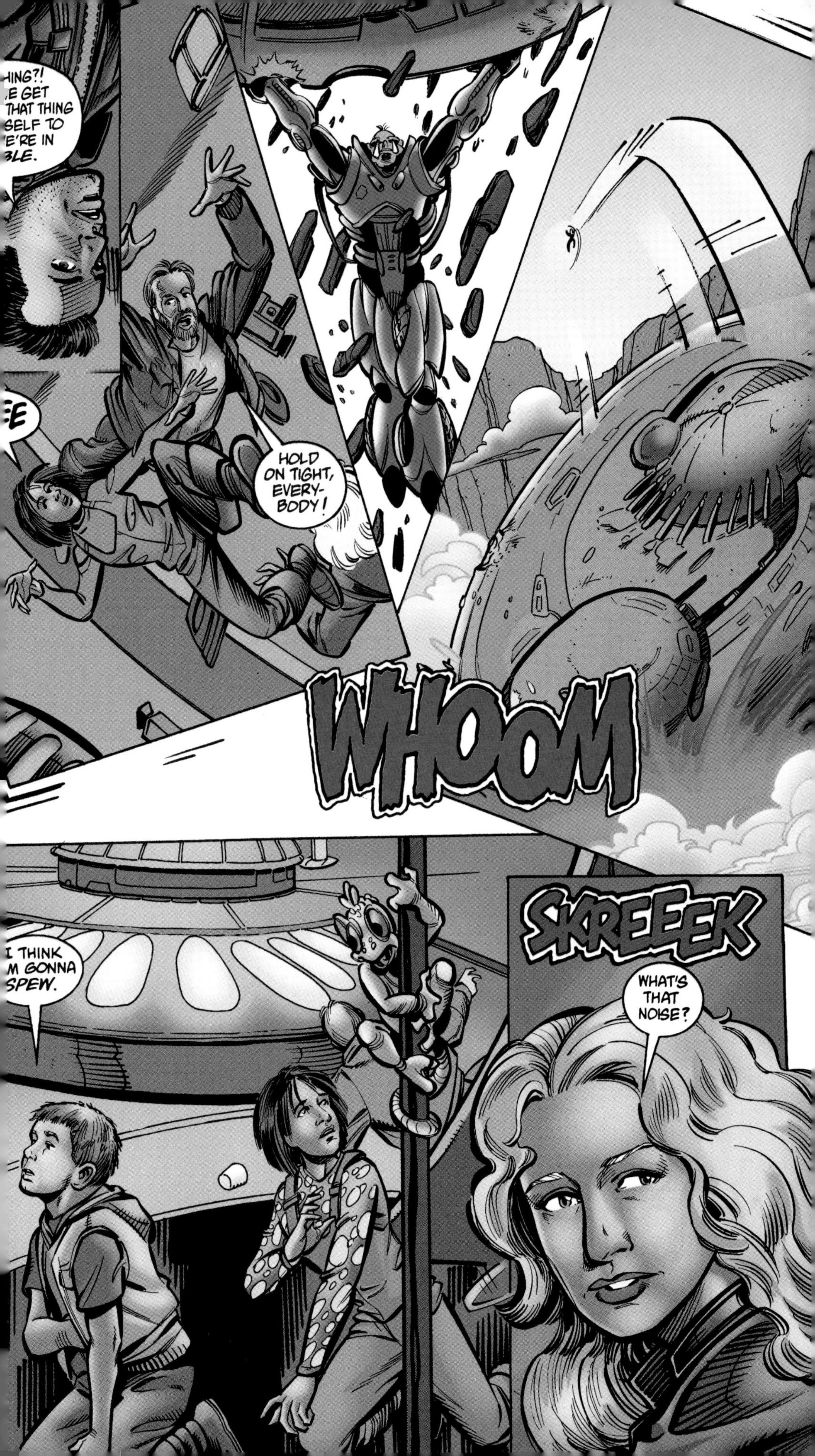

HING?! E GET THAT THING SELF TO E'RE IN BLE.
HOLD ON TIGHT, EVERY-BODY!
WHOOM
I THINK M GONNA SPEW.
SKREEEK
WHAT'S THAT NOISE?

SREEUUUUNK!
EEEEEE
SMITH, IS THAT STILL YO IN THERE?
SMITH PROFESSOR.
I DON'T KNOW WHAT'S GOING ON WITH HIM, BUT THIS MIGHT BE A GOOD TIME TO ESCAPE TO THE OUTSIDE. I WANT EVERYONE TO GRAB WHAT-EVER SUPPLIES YOU CAN CARRY.
LEAVE THE SHIP? A YOU NUTS?! DON'T WE JU GIVE HIM TH KEYS?
DON, I WILL ARGUE WITH YOU LATER, BUT RIGHT NOW--LET'S GO!

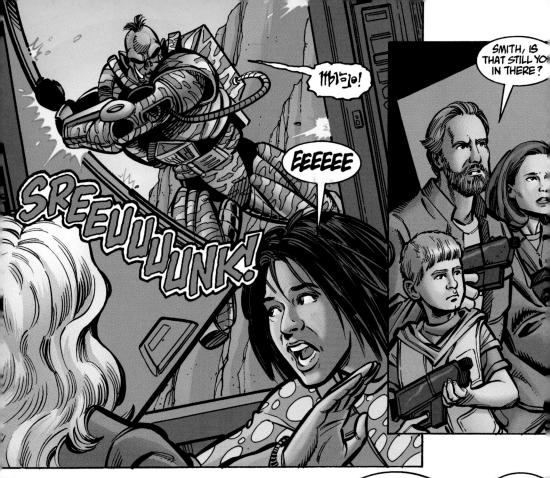

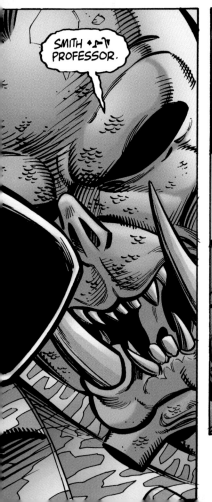

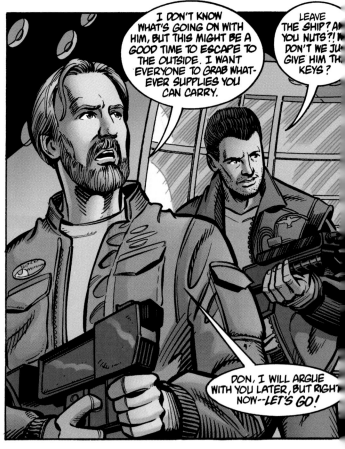

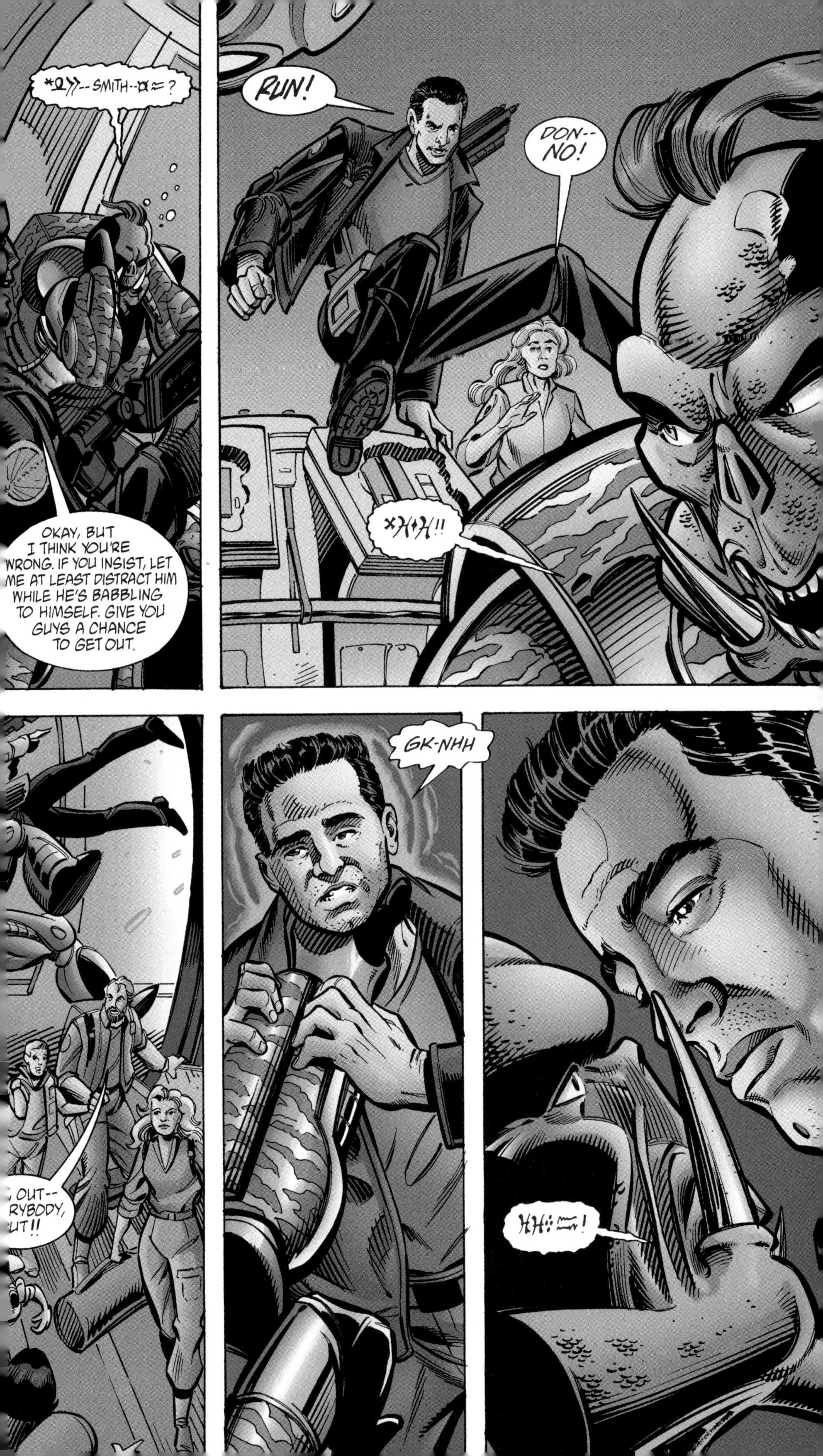

SMITH
OKAY, BUT I THINK YOU'RE WRONG. IF YOU INSIST, LET ME AT LEAST DISTRACT HIM WHILE HE'S BABBLING TO HIMSELF. GIVE YOU GUYS A CHANCE TO GET OUT.
RUN!
DON-- NO!
OUT-- RYBODY, UT!!
GK-NHH

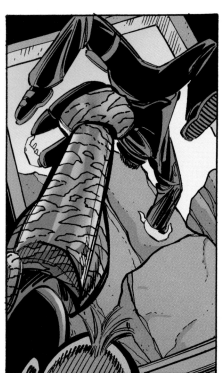

SLAM

HNK

YOU ALL RIGHT? THAT WAS STUPID--YOU COULD HAVE BEEN *KILLED*.

I'M FINE-- I'VE BEEN HURT WORSE.

I'M NOT SURPRISED. NOTHING COULD CRACK YOUR THICK SKULL.

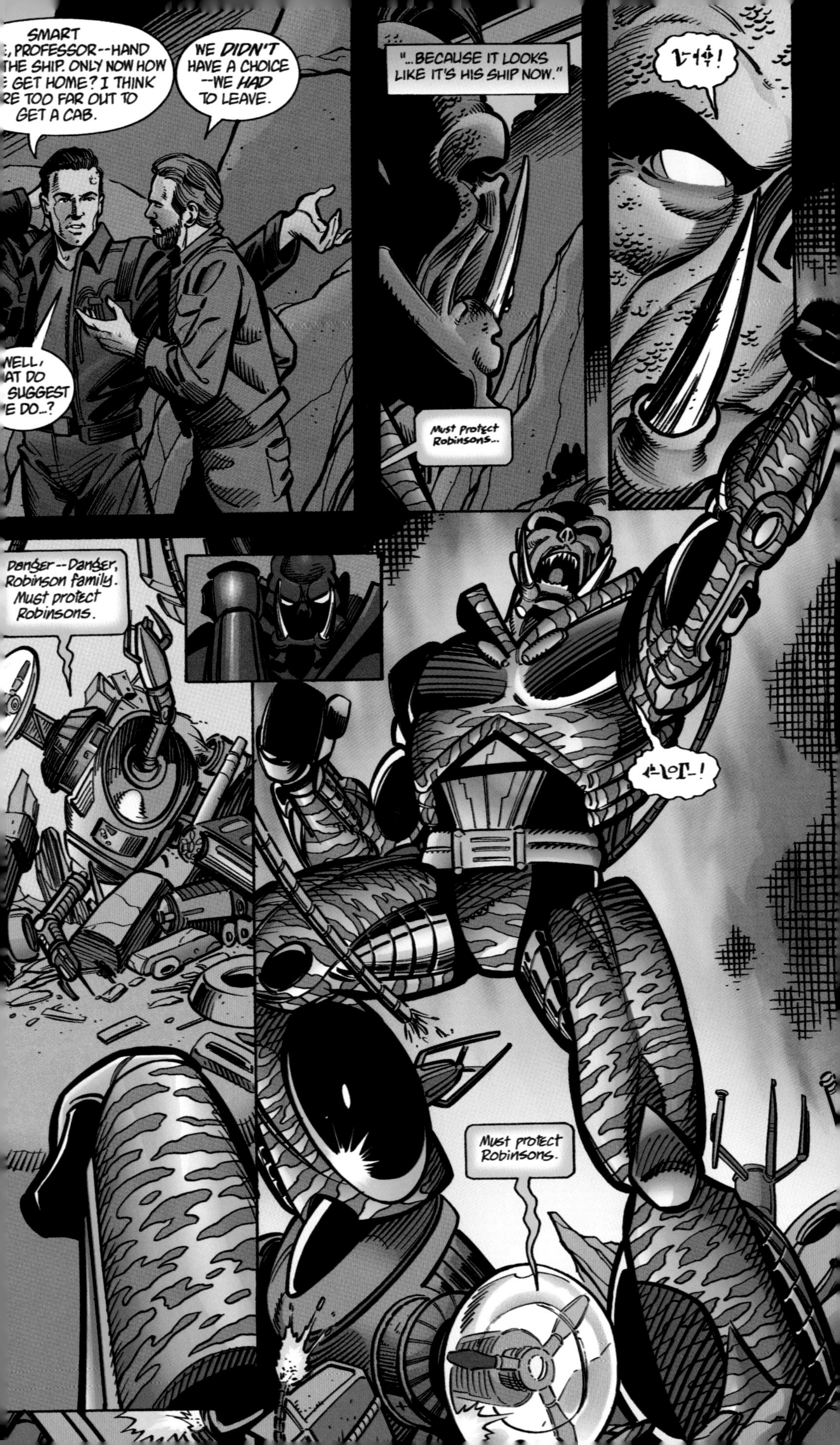
SMART
E, PROFESSOR--HAND
THE SHIP. ONLY NOW HOW
E GET HOME? I THINK
RE TOO FAR OUT TO
GET A CAB.
WE *DIDN'T* HAVE A CHOICE --WE *HAD* TO LEAVE.
WELL,
AT DO
SUGGEST
E DO...?
"...BECAUSE IT LOOKS LIKE IT'S HIS SHIP NOW."
Must protect Robinsons...
Danger--Danger, Robinson family. Must protect Robinsons.
Must protect Robinsons.

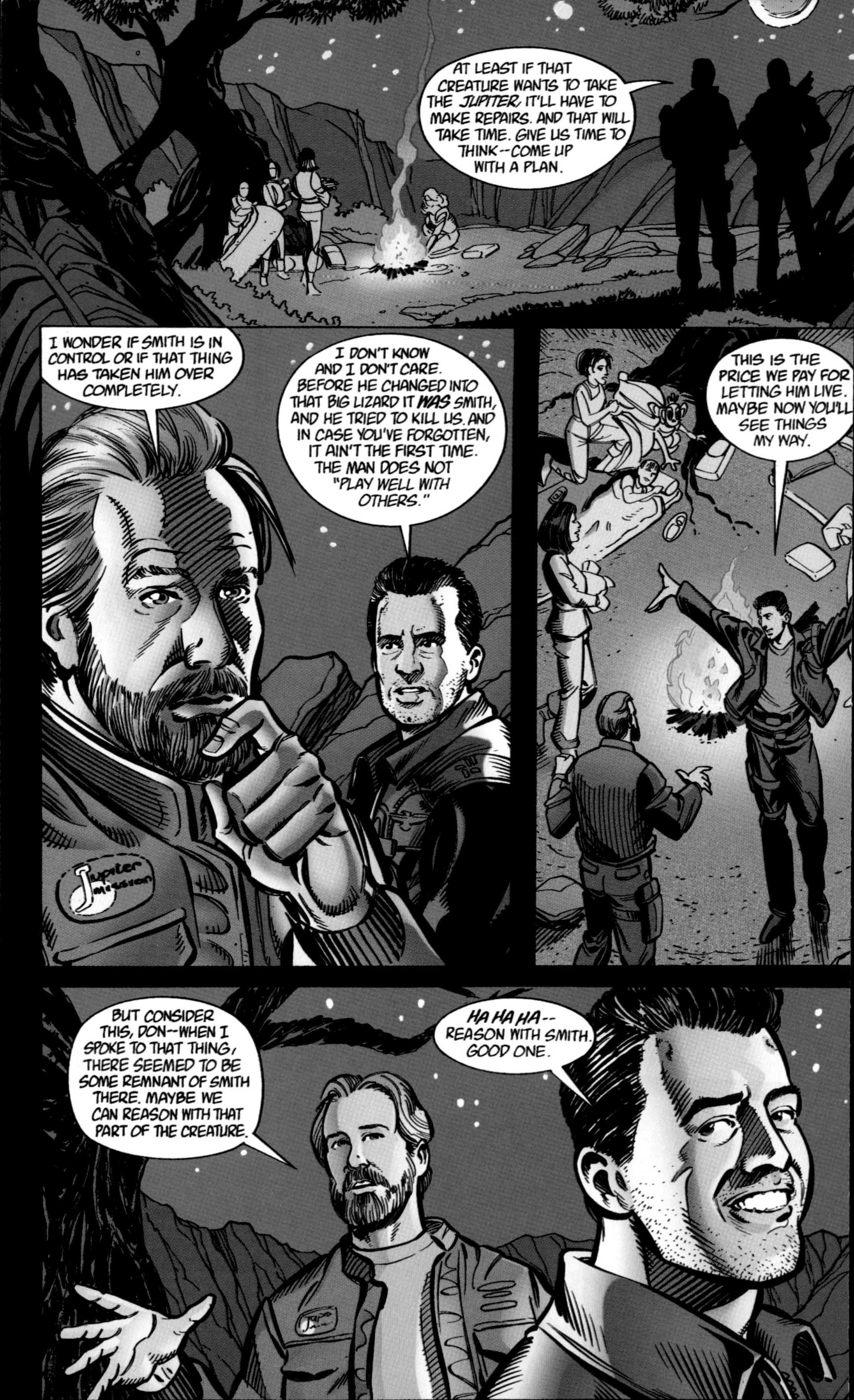
AT LEAST IF THAT CREATURE WANTS TO TAKE THE JUPITER, IT'LL HAVE TO MAKE REPAIRS. AND THAT WILL TAKE TIME. GIVE US TIME TO THINK--COME UP WITH A PLAN.
I WONDER IF SMITH IS IN CONTROL OR IF THAT THING HAS TAKEN HIM OVER COMPLETELY.
I DON'T KNOW AND I DON'T CARE. BEFORE HE CHANGED INTO THAT BIG LIZARD IT WAS SMITH, AND HE TRIED TO KILL US. AND IN CASE YOU'VE FORGOTTEN, IT AIN'T THE FIRST TIME. THE MAN DOES NOT "PLAY WELL WITH OTHERS."
Jupiter mission
THIS IS THE PRICE WE PAY FOR LETTING HIM LIVE. MAYBE NOW YOU'LL SEE THINGS MY WAY.
BUT CONSIDER THIS, DON--WHEN I SPOKE TO THAT THING, THERE SEEMED TO BE SOME REMNANT OF SMITH THERE. MAYBE WE CAN REASON WITH THAT PART OF THE CREATURE.
HA HA HA-- REASON WITH SMITH. GOOD ONE.

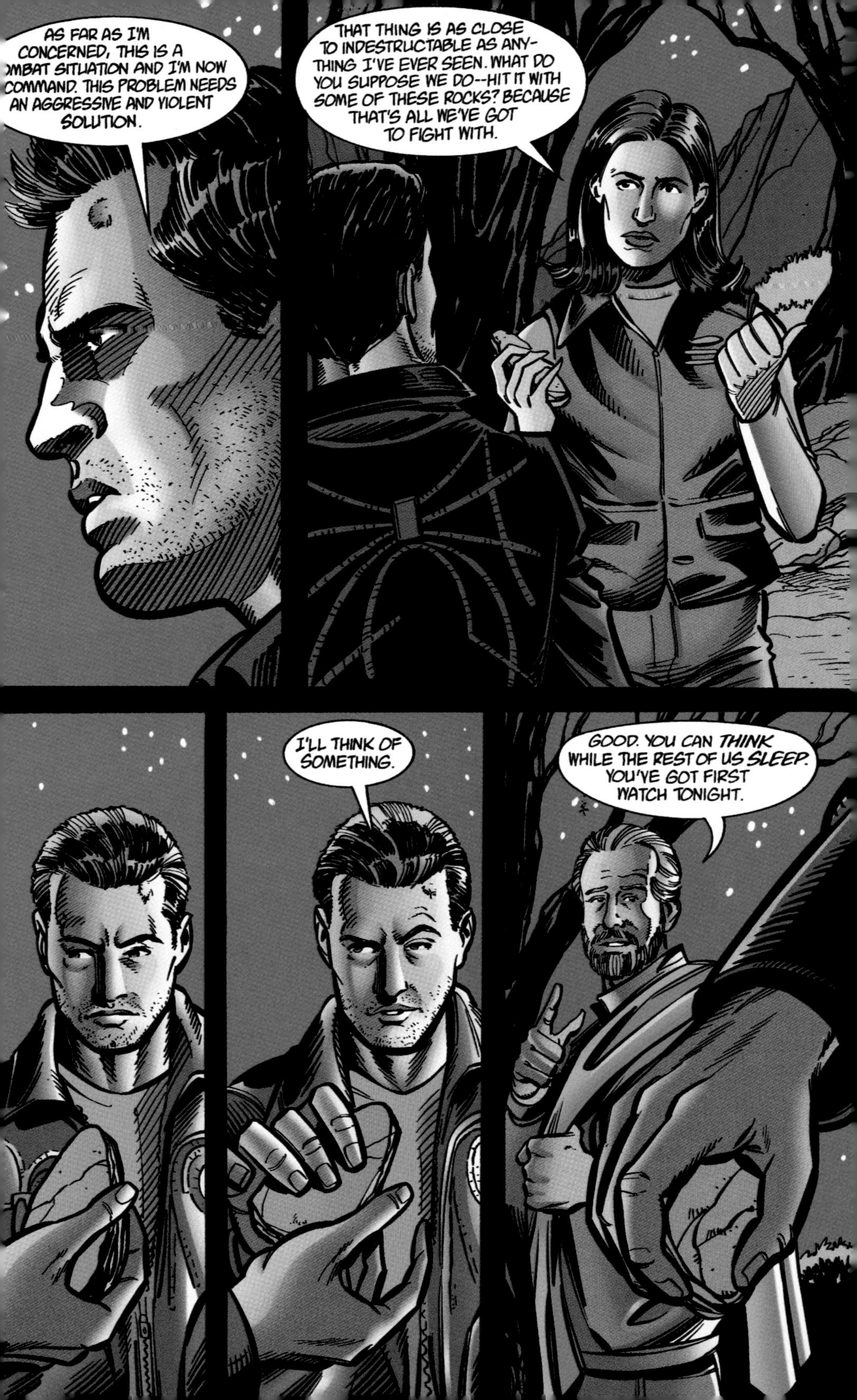

AS FAR AS I'M CONCERNED, THIS IS A OMBAT SITUATION AND I'M NOW COMMAND. THIS PROBLEM NEEDS AN AGGRESSIVE AND VIOLENT SOLUTION.
THAT THING IS AS CLOSE TO INDESTRUCTABLE AS ANY-THING I'VE EVER SEEN. WHAT DO YOU SUPPOSE WE DO--HIT IT WITH SOME OF THESE ROCKS? BECAUSE THAT'S ALL WE'VE GOT TO FIGHT WITH.
I'LL THINK OF SOMETHING.
GOOD. YOU CAN THINK WHILE THE REST OF US SLEEP. YOU'VE GOT FIRST WATCH TONIGHT.

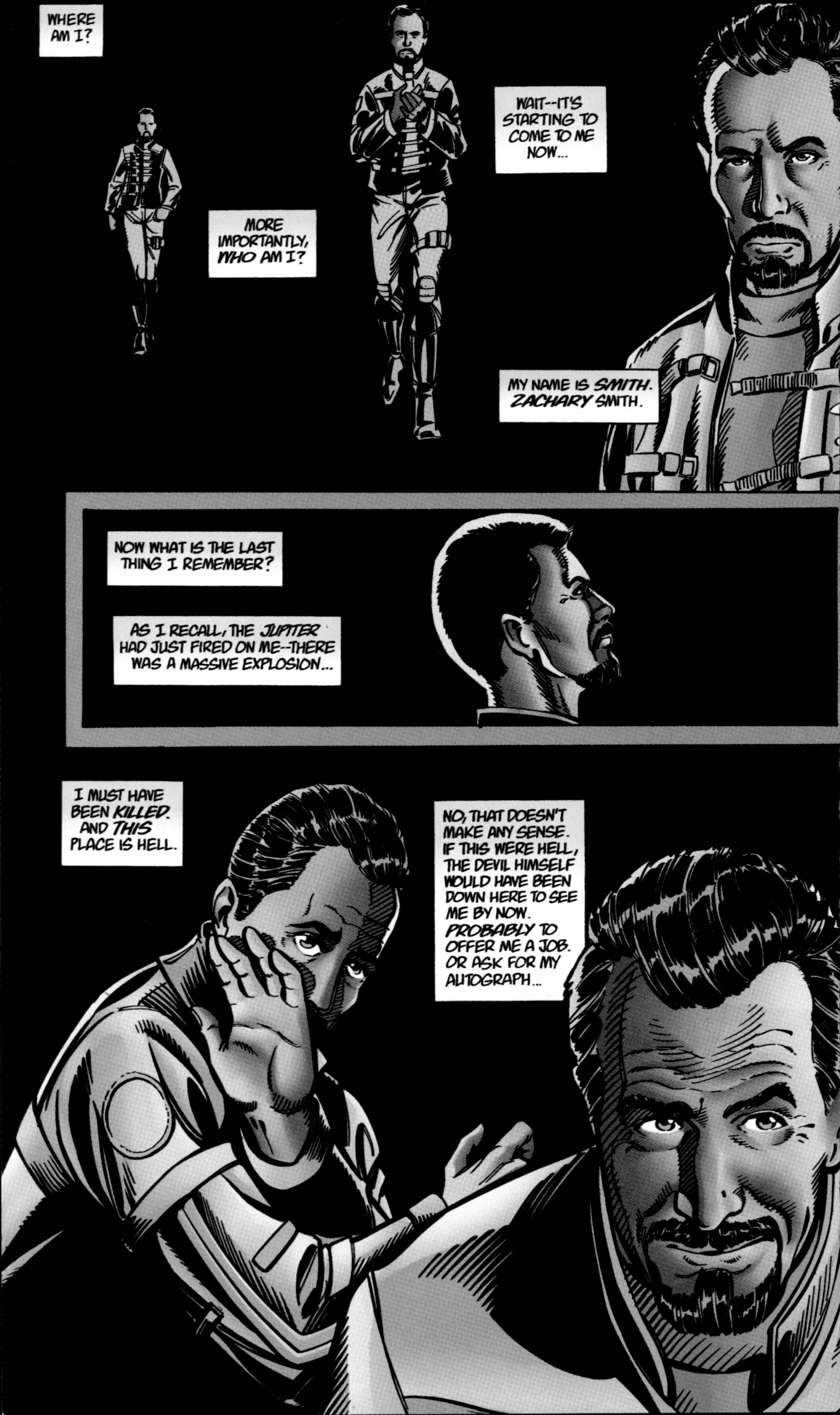
WHERE AM I?
MORE IMPORTANTLY, WHO AM I?
WAIT--IT'S STARTING TO COME TO ME NOW...
MY NAME IS SMITH. ZACHARY SMITH.
NOW WHAT IS THE LAST THING I REMEMBER?
AS I RECALL, THE JUPITER HAD JUST FIRED ON ME--THERE WAS A MASSIVE EXPLOSION...
I MUST HAVE BEEN KILLED. AND THIS PLACE IS HELL.
NO, THAT DOESN'T MAKE ANY SENSE. IF THIS WERE HELL, THE DEVIL HIMSELF WOULD HAVE BEEN DOWN HERE TO SEE ME BY NOW. PROBABLY TO OFFER ME A JOB. OR ASK FOR MY AUTOGRAPH...

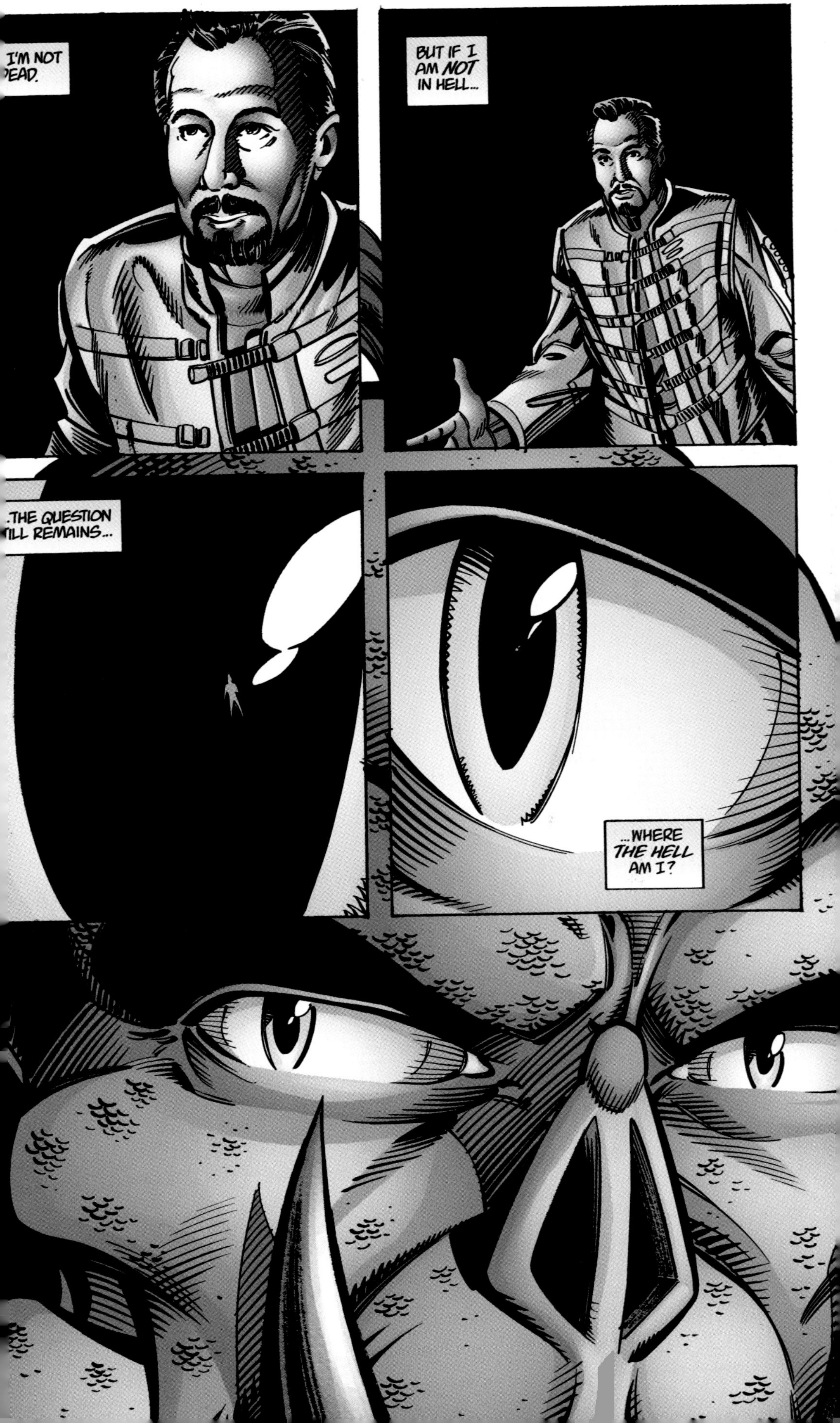
I'M NOT
PEAD.
BUT IF I
AM *NOT*
IN HELL...
.THE QUESTION
ILL REMAINS...
...WHERE
THE HELL
AM I?

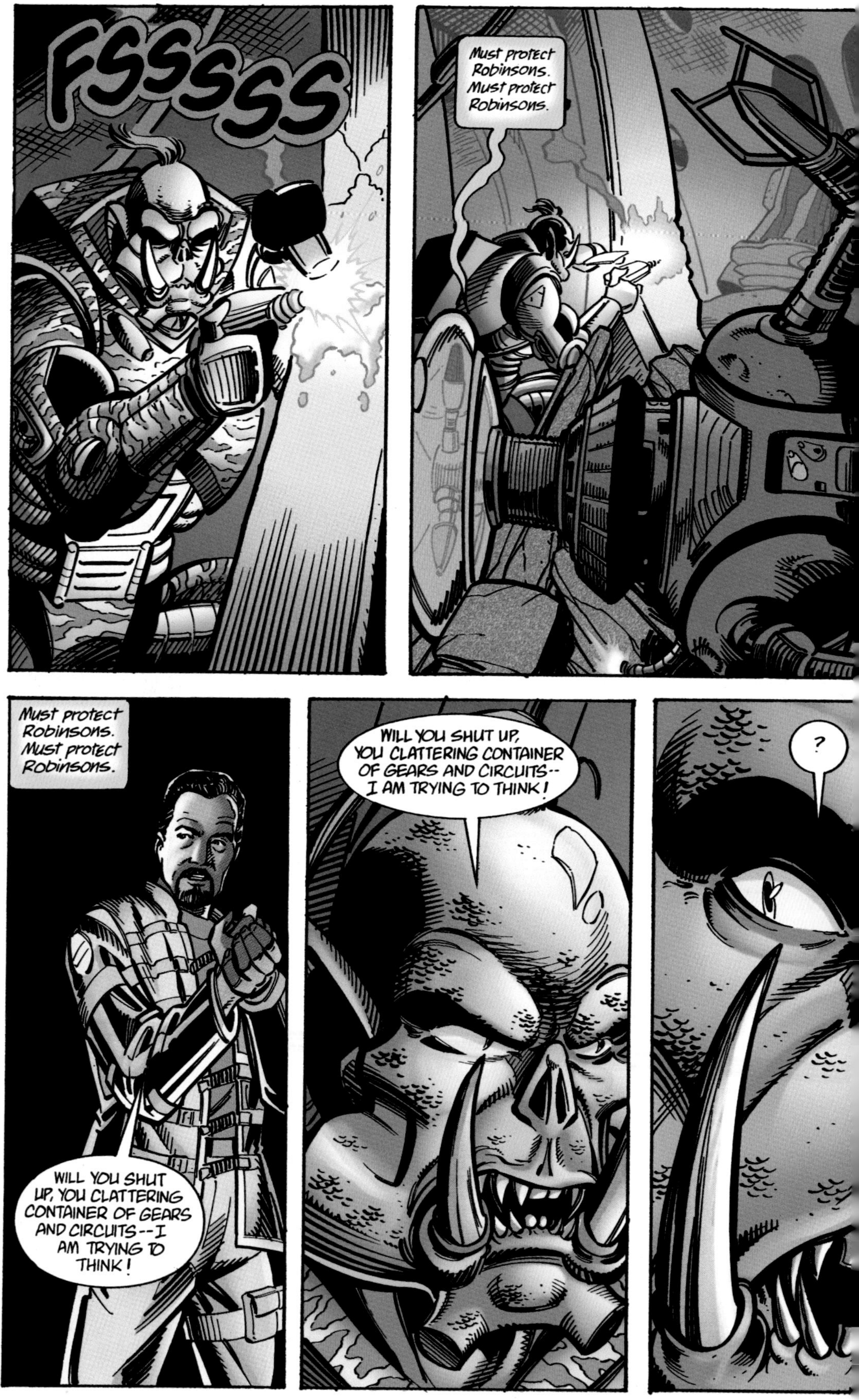
FSSSSS
Must protect Robinsons. Must protect Robinsons.
Must protect Robinsons. Must protect Robinsons.
WILL YOU SHUT UP, YOU CLATTERING CONTAINER OF GEARS AND CIRCUITS--I AM TRYING TO THINK!
WILL YOU SHUT UP, YOU CLATTERING CONTAINER OF GEARS AND CIRCUITS--I AM TRYING TO THINK!
?

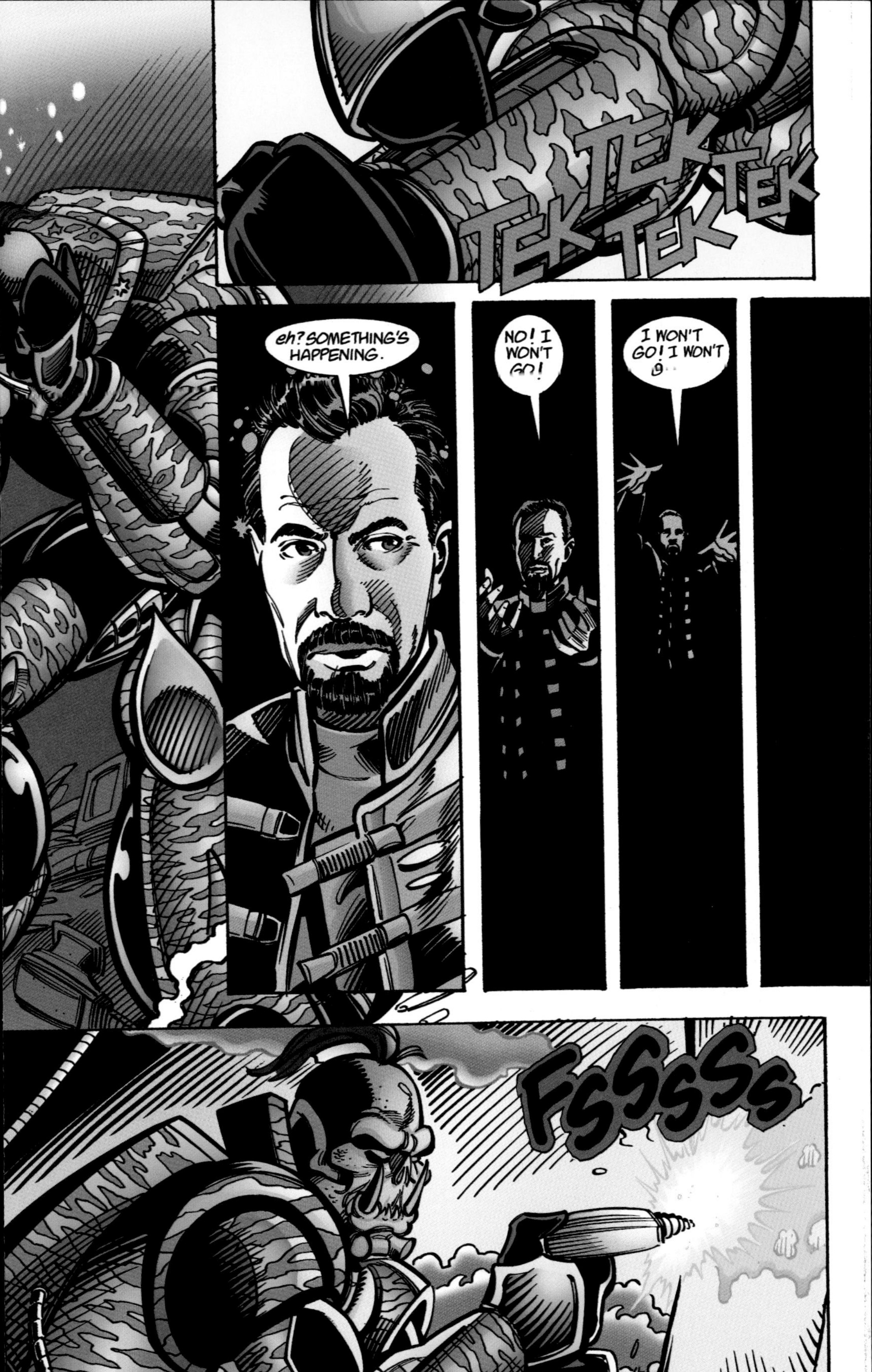
TEK TEK TEK TEK
eh? SOMETHING'S HAPPENING.
NO! I WON'T GO!
I WON'T GO! I WON'T g...
FsSSsSs

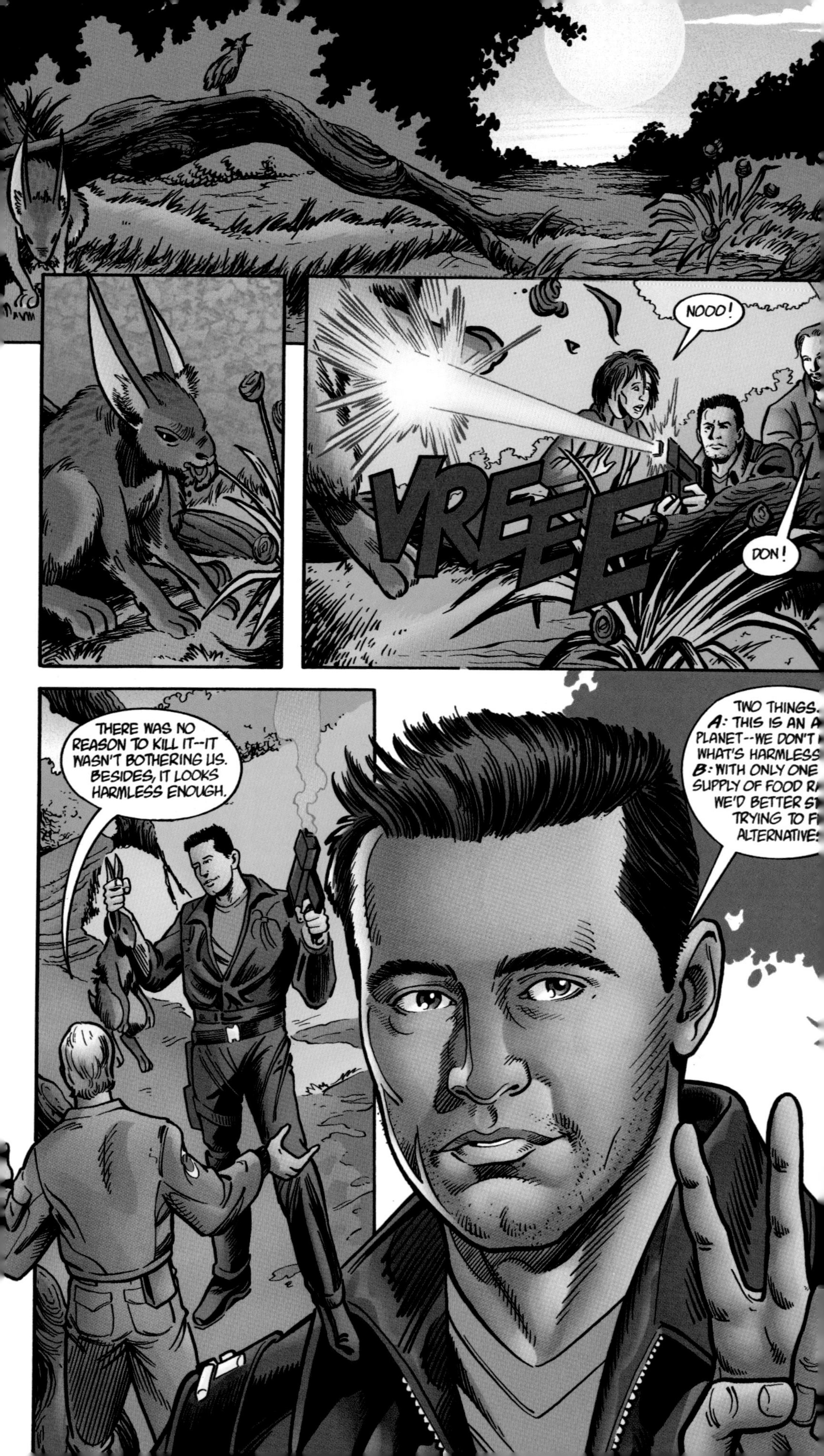
NOOO!
VREEEE
DON!
THERE WAS NO REASON TO KILL IT--IT WASN'T BOTHERING US. BESIDES, IT LOOKS HARMLESS ENOUGH.
TWO THINGS. A: THIS IS AN
PLANET--WE DON'T
WHAT'S
B: WITH ONLY ONE
SUPPLY OF FOOD
WE'D BETTER
TRYING TO

GUESS YOU'RE RIGHT. WE'D [?] THINK OF SOMETHING. ANY IDEAS [?]UT HOW TO GET THE SHIP BACK?

ZILCH. AS LONG AS THAT THING HAS THE SUIT ON, THERE'S NO WAY TO FIGHT IT--*UNLESS*...

jupiter two

john robinson

SWAP!

OF COURSE! WHY DIDN'T I THINK OF IT BEFORE? I'M SO *STUPID!*

[?]MITTING THAT [?]AVE A PROBLEM [?]E FIRST STEP, DON. [?] PROUD OF YOU.

CUTE.

BOY, YOU STEPPED RIGHT INTO THAT ONE, DIDN'T YOU? SO WHAT'S YOUR IDEA?

DOCTOR SMITH GOT A HOLD OF THAT SUIT AFTER HE FELL DOWN THAT HOLE. MAYBE THERE'S ANOTHER SUIT DOWN THERE OR SOMETHING.

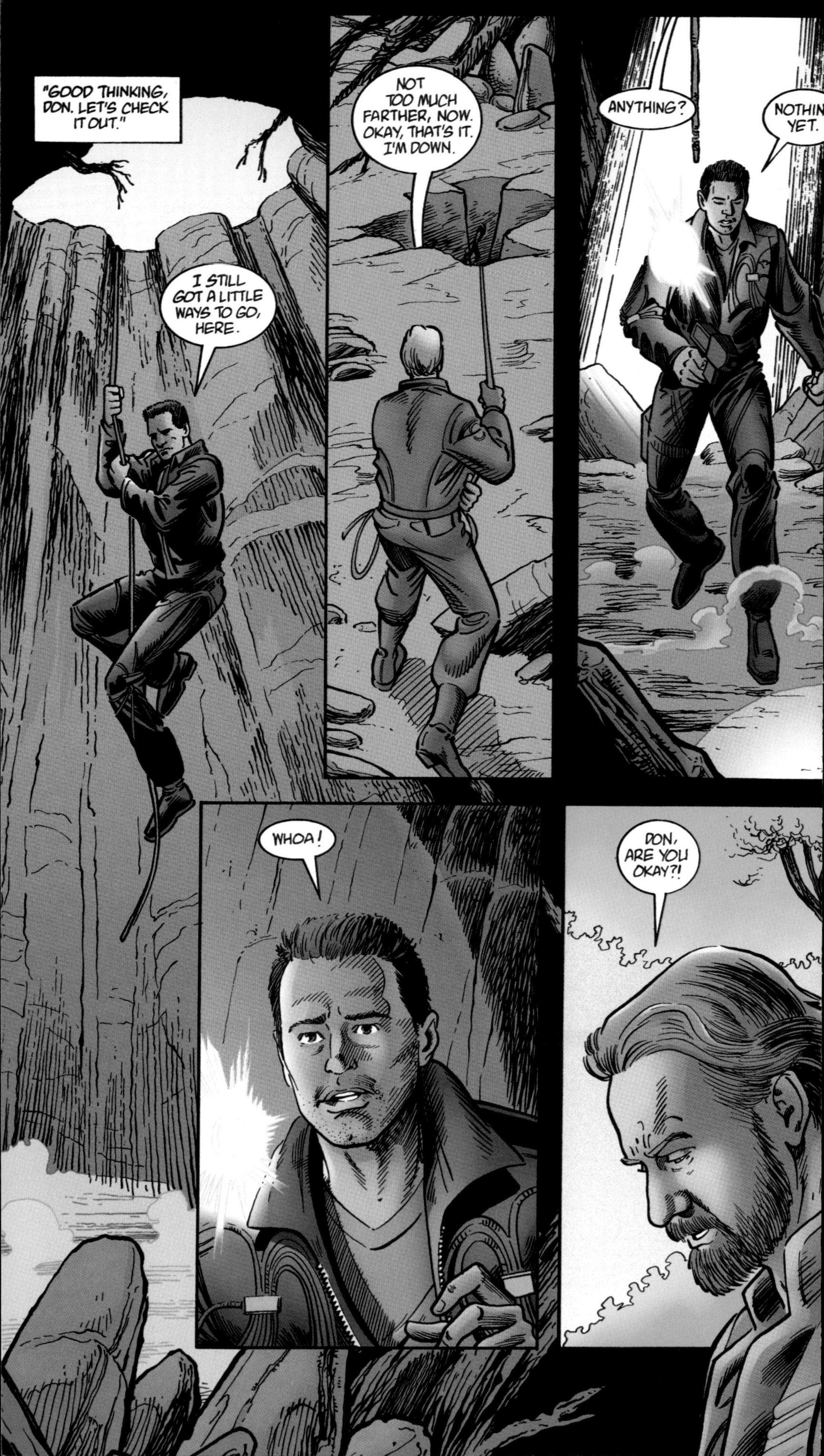
"GOOD THINKING, DON. LET'S CHECK IT OUT."
I STILL GOT A LITTLE WAYS TO GO, HERE.
NOT TOO MUCH FARTHER, NOW. OKAY, THAT'S IT. I'M DOWN.
ANYTHING?
NOTHIN YET.
WHOA!
DON, ARE YOU OKAY?!

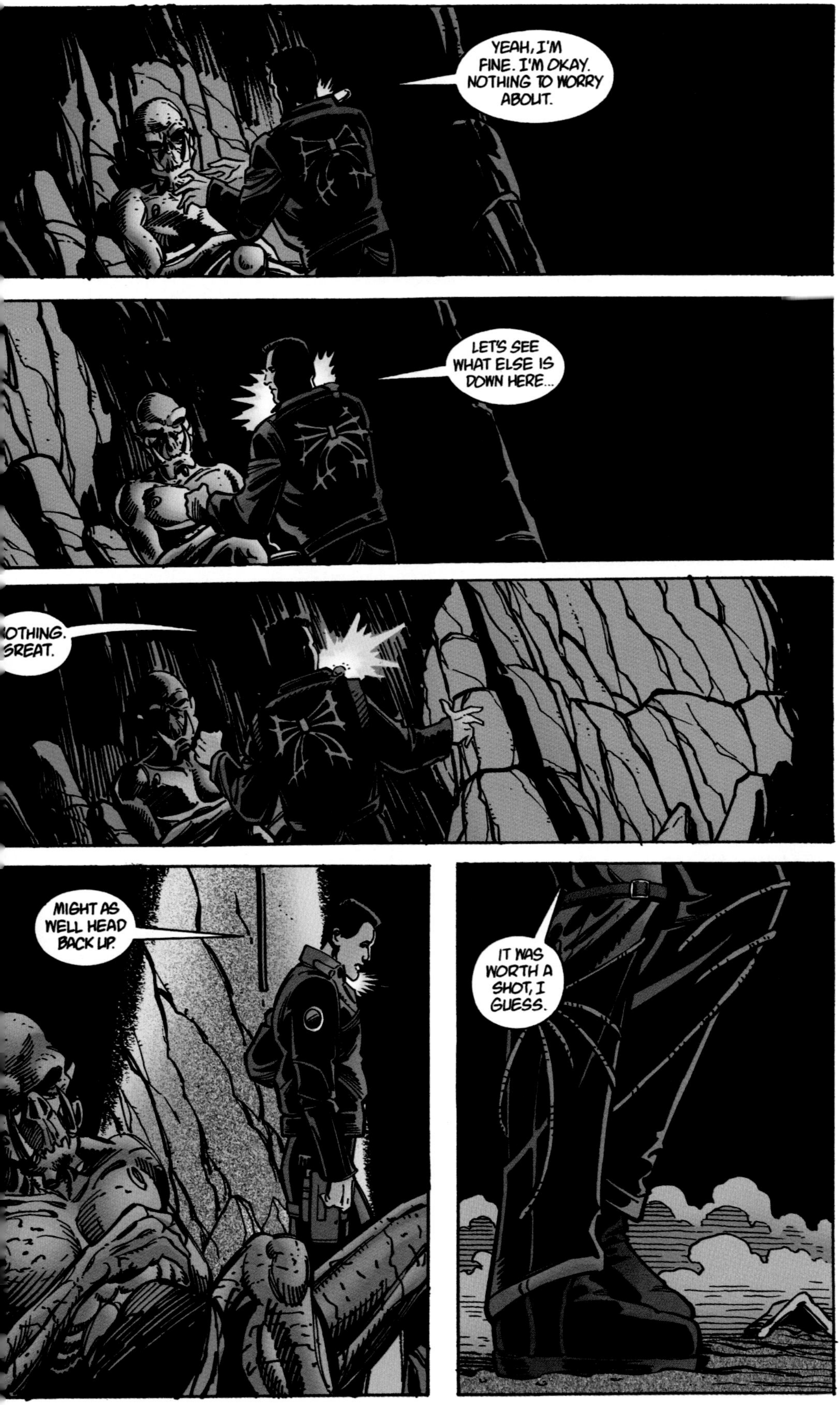
YEAH, I'M FINE. I'M OKAY. NOTHING TO WORRY ABOUT.
LET'S SEE WHAT ELSE IS DOWN HERE...
OTHING. REAT.
MIGHT AS WELL HEAD BACK UP.
IT WAS WORTH A SHOT, I GUESS.

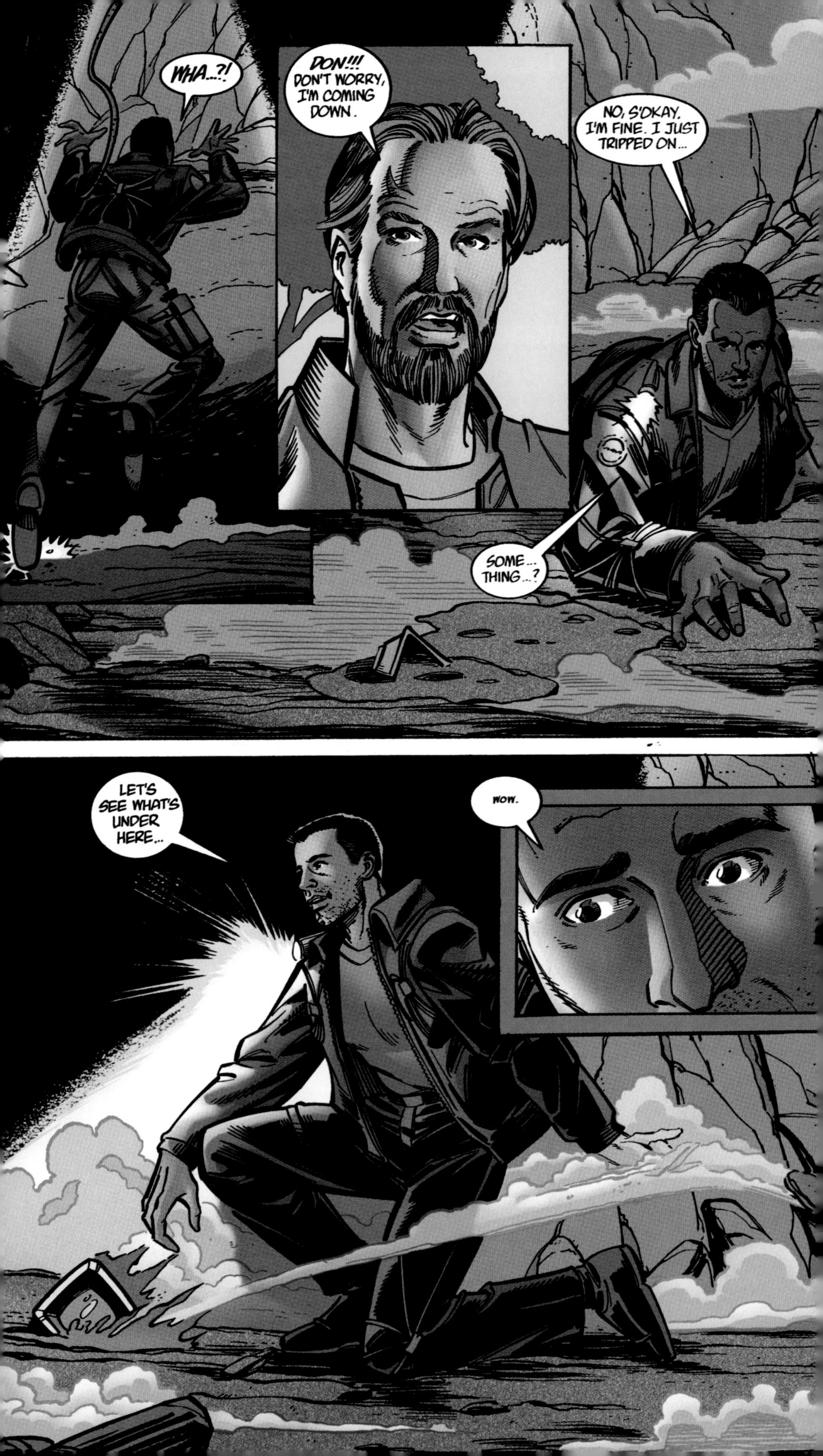
WHA...?!
DON!!! DON'T WORRY, I'M COMING DOWN.
NO, S'OKAY. I'M FINE. I JUST TRIPPED ON...
SOME... THING...?
LET'S SEE WHAT'S UNDER HERE...
WOW.

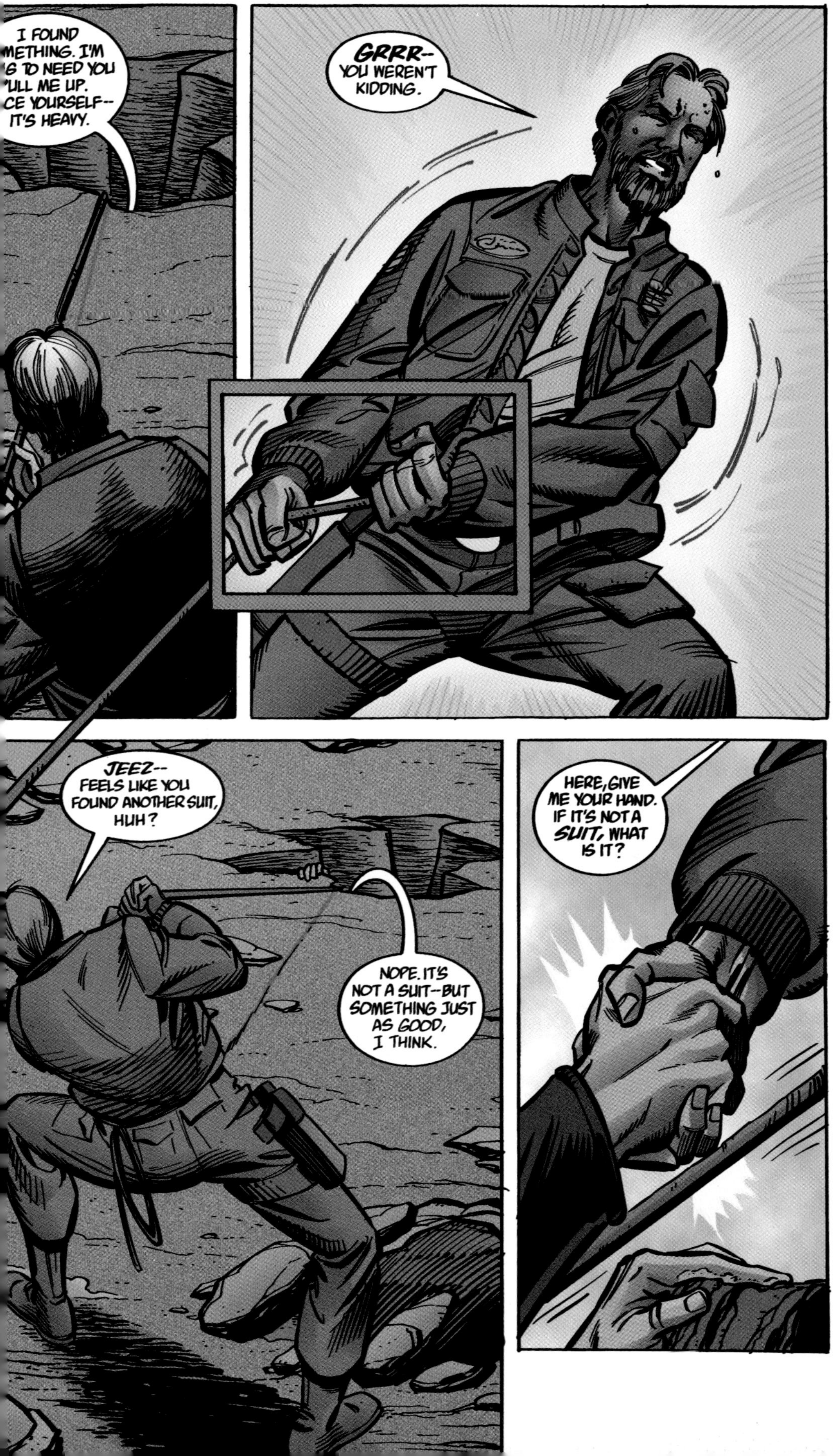
I FOUND METHING. I'M G TO NEED YOU ULL ME UP. CE YOURSELF-- IT'S HEAVY.
GRRR-- YOU WEREN'T KIDDING.
JEEZ-- FEELS LIKE YOU FOUND ANOTHER SUIT, HUH?
NOPE. IT'S NOT A SUIT--BUT SOMETHING JUST AS GOOD, I THINK.
HERE, GIVE ME YOUR HAND. IF IT'S NOT A SUIT, WHAT IS IT?

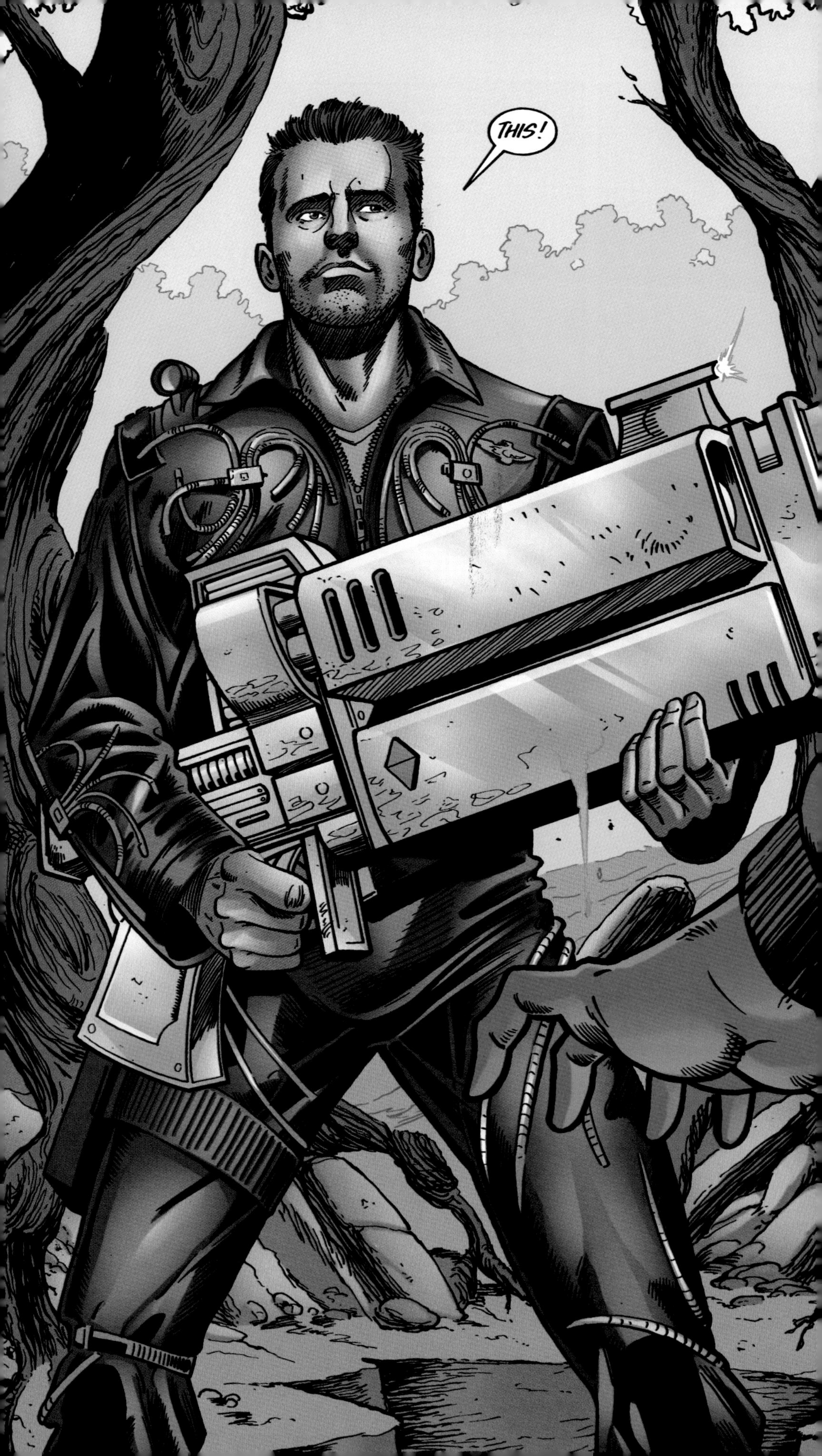
THIS!

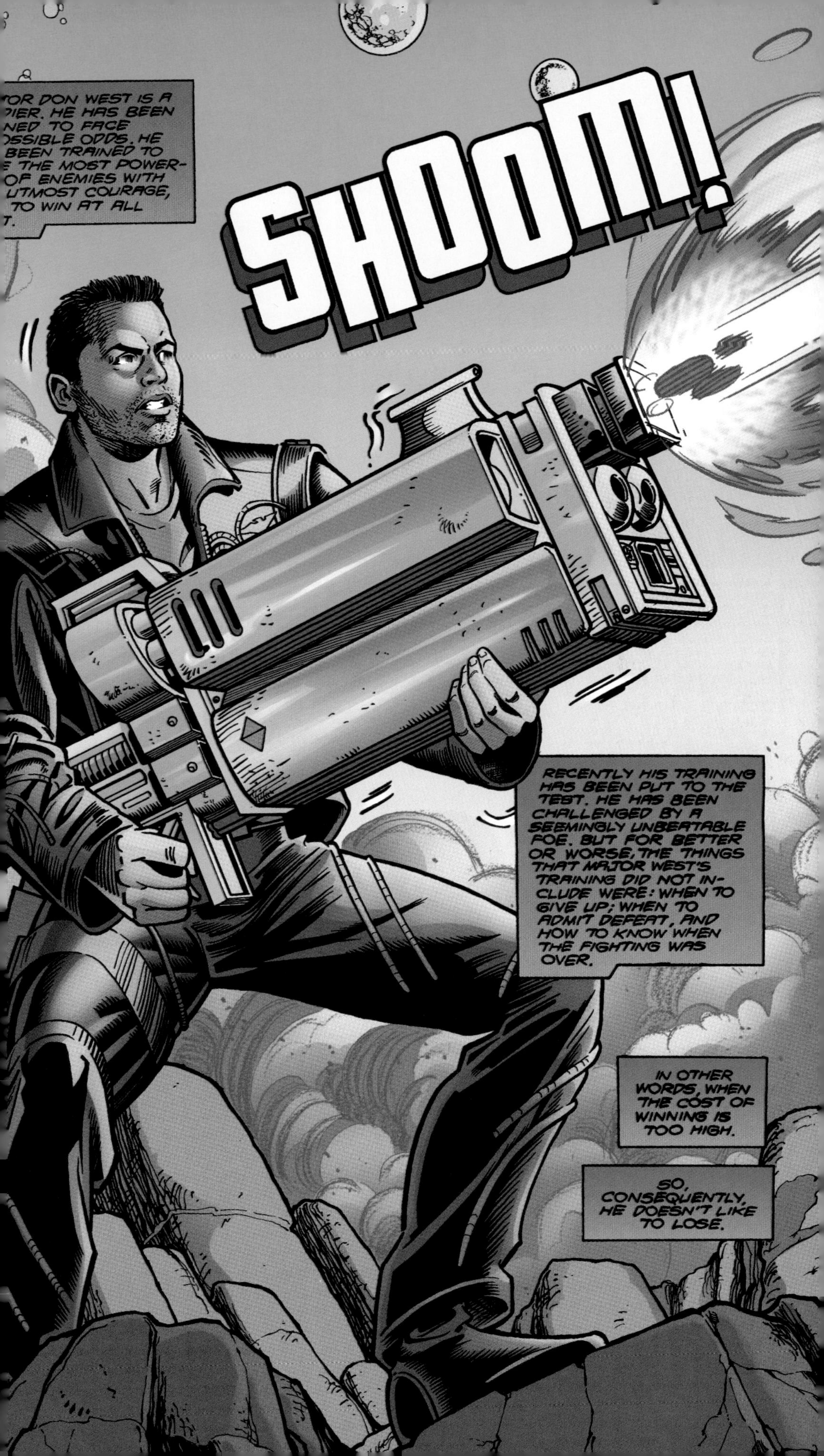

OR DON WEST IS A
DIER. HE HAS BEEN
NED TO FACE
OSSIBLE ODDS. HE
BEEN TRAINED TO
E THE MOST POWER-
OF ENEMIES WITH
UTMOST COURAGE,
TO WIN AT ALL
T.
SHOOM!
RECENTLY HIS TRAINING HAS BEEN PUT TO THE TEST. HE HAS BEEN CHALLENGED BY A SEEMINGLY UNBEATABLE FOE. BUT FOR BETTER OR WORSE, THE THINGS THAT MAJOR WEST'S TRAINING DID NOT INCLUDE WERE: WHEN TO GIVE UP; WHEN TO ADMIT DEFEAT, AND HOW TO KNOW WHEN THE FIGHTING WAS OVER.
IN OTHER WORDS, WHEN THE COST OF WINNING IS TOO HIGH.
SO, CONSEQUENTLY, HE DOESN'T LIKE TO LOSE.

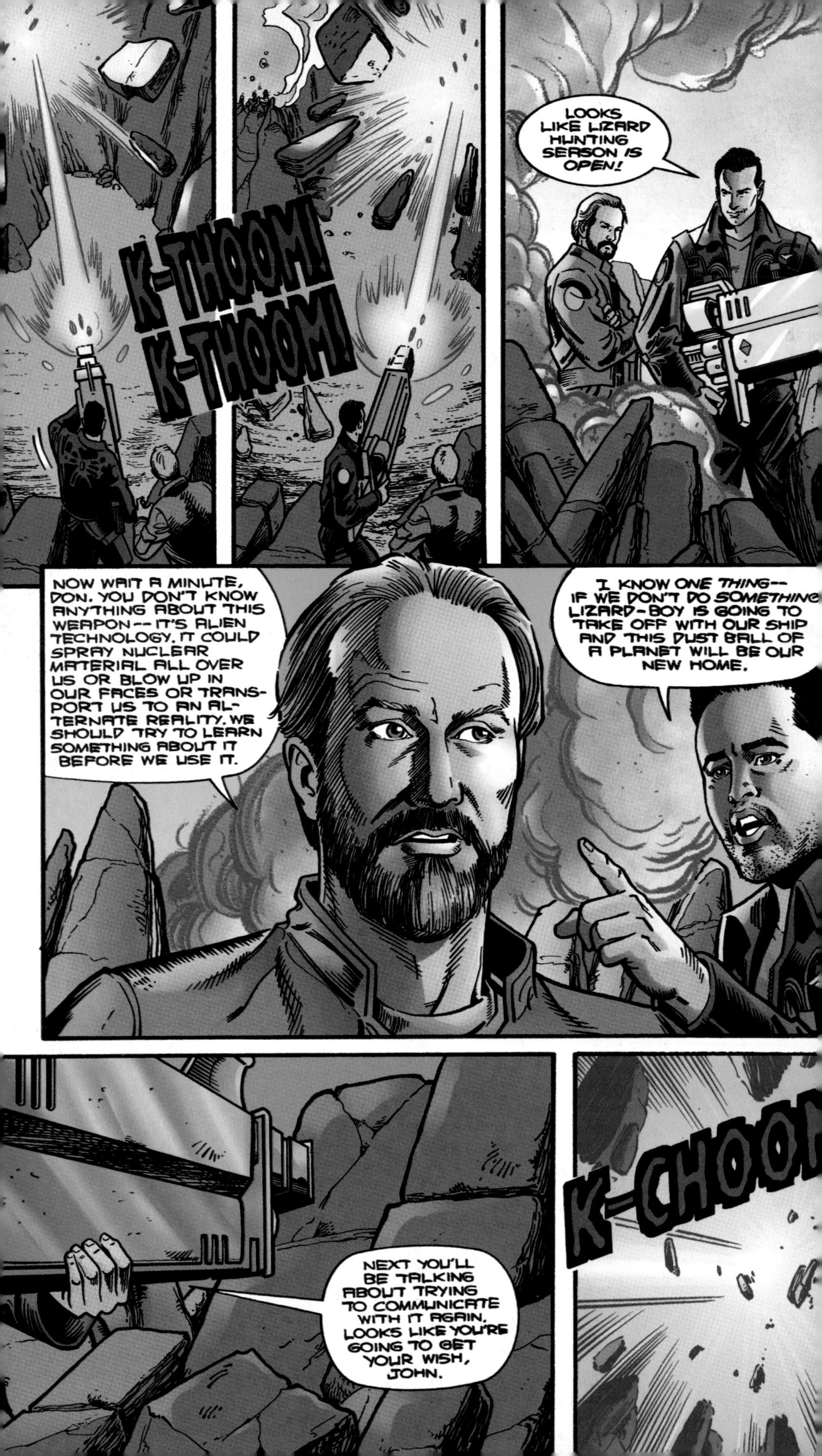
K-THOOM!
K-THOOM!
LOOKS LIKE LIZARD HUNTING SEASON IS OPEN!
NOW WAIT A MINUTE, DON. YOU DON'T KNOW ANYTHING ABOUT THIS WEAPON -- IT'S ALIEN TECHNOLOGY. IT COULD SPRAY NUCLEAR MATERIAL ALL OVER US OR BLOW UP IN OUR FACES OR TRANSPORT US TO AN ALTERNATE REALITY. WE SHOULD TRY TO LEARN SOMETHING ABOUT IT BEFORE WE USE IT.
I KNOW ONE THING-- IF WE DON'T DO SOMETHING LIZARD-BOY IS GOING TO TAKE OFF WITH OUR SHIP AND THIS DUST BALL OF A PLANET WILL BE OUR NEW HOME.
NEXT YOU'LL BE TALKING ABOUT TRYING TO COMMUNICATE WITH IT AGAIN. LOOKS LIKE YOU'RE GOING TO GET YOUR WISH, JOHN.

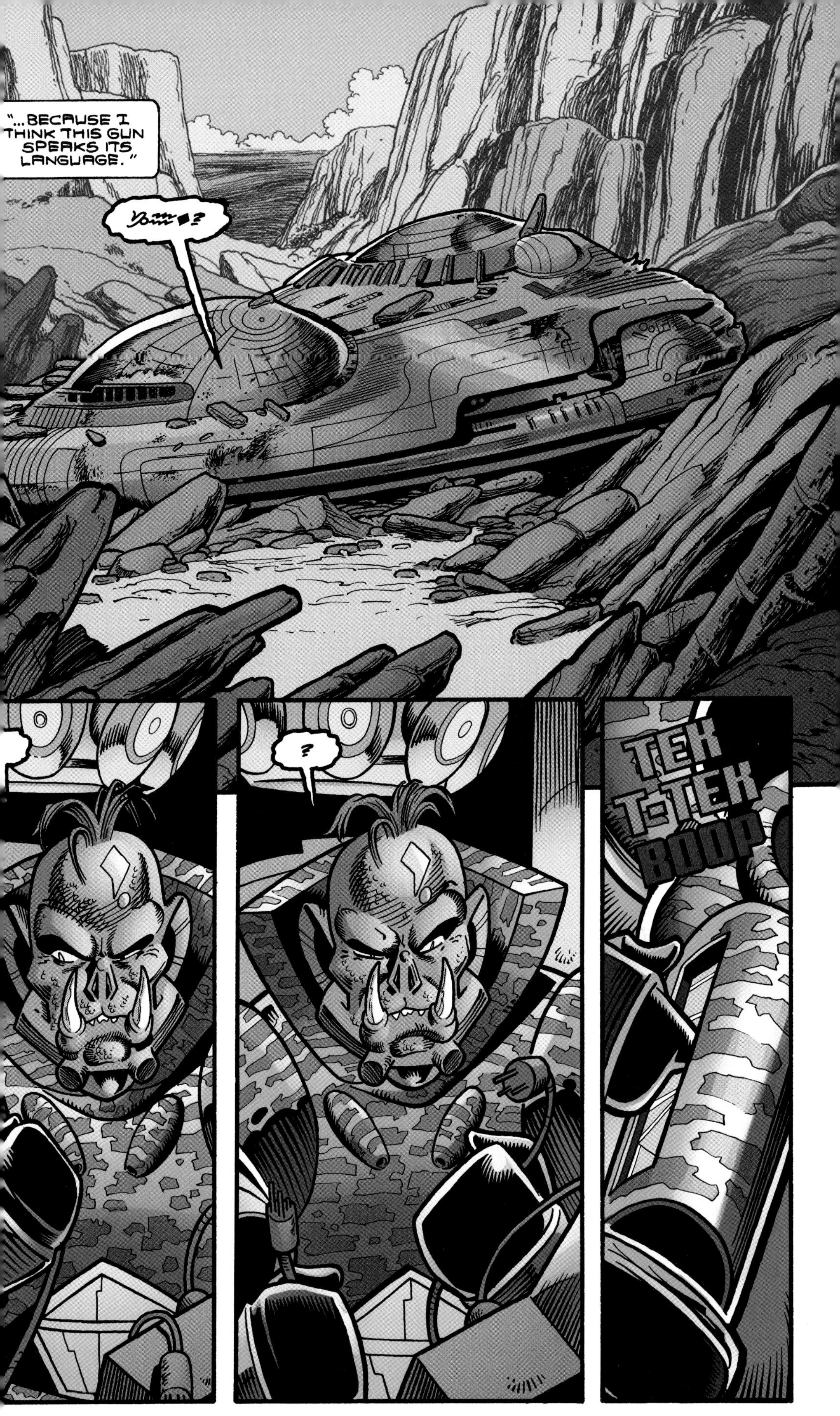
"...BECAUSE I THINK THIS GUN SPEAKS ITS LANGUAGE."
?
TEK T-TEK BOOP

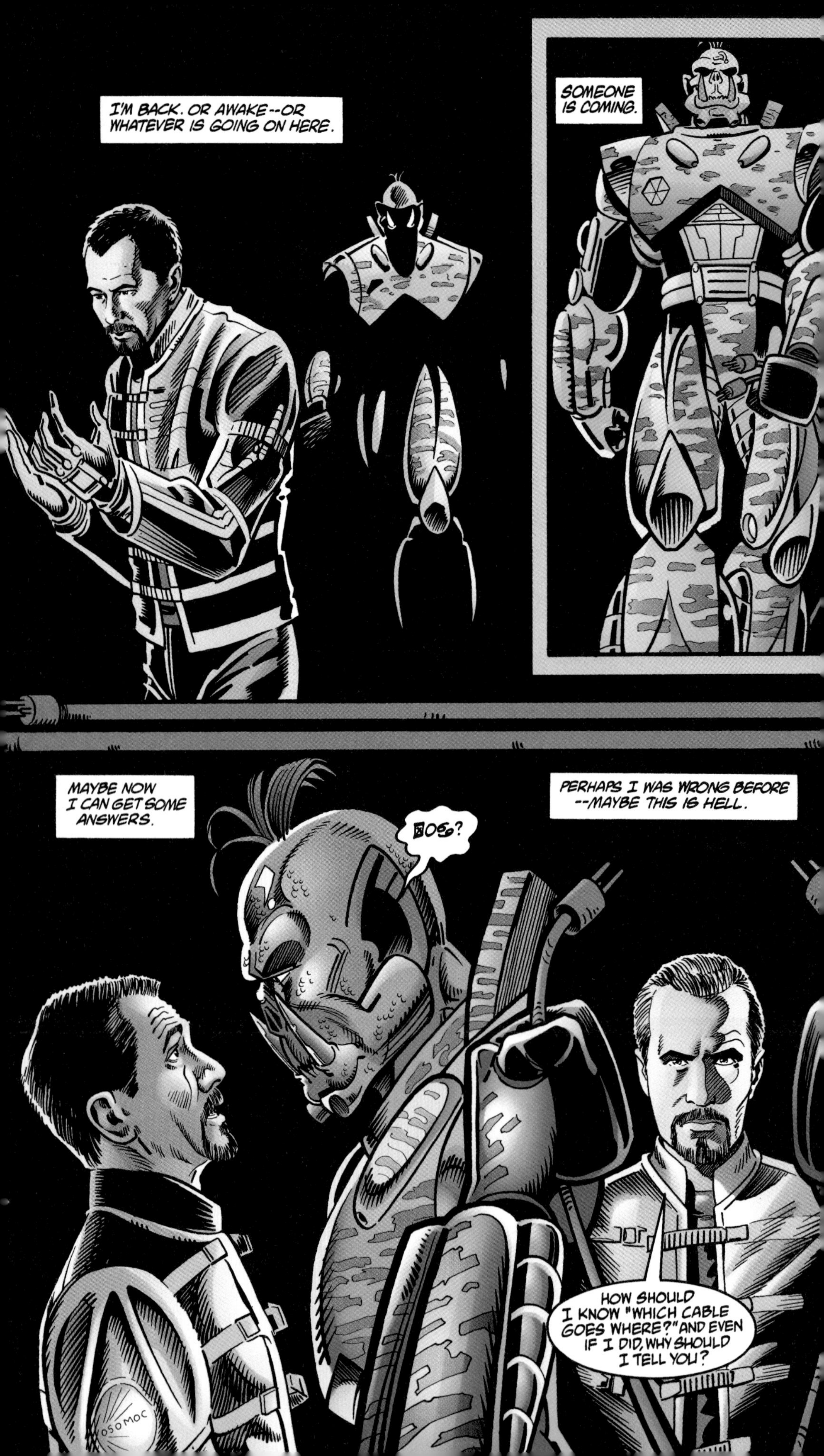
I'M BACK. OR AWAKE--OR WHATEVER IS GOING ON HERE.
SOMEONE IS COMING.
MAYBE NOW I CAN GET SOME ANSWERS.
PERHAPS I WAS WRONG BEFORE --MAYBE THIS IS HELL.
HOW SHOULD I KNOW "WHICH CABLE GOES WHERE?" AND EVEN IF I DID, WHY SHOULD I TELL YOU?

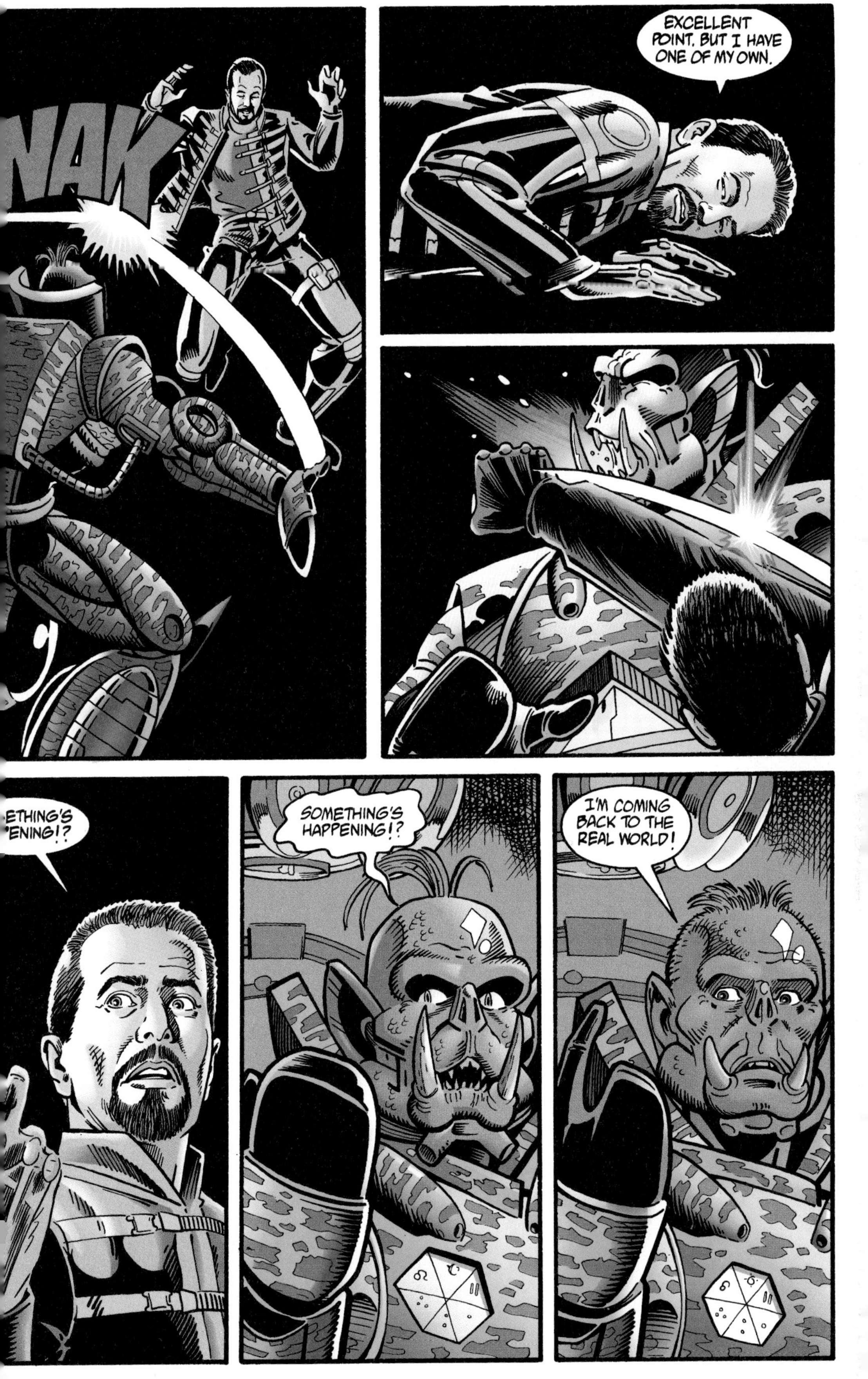
NAK
EXCELLENT POINT. BUT I HAVE ONE OF MY OWN.
ETHING'S 'ENING!?
SOMETHING'S HAPPENING!?
I'M COMING BACK TO THE REAL WORLD!

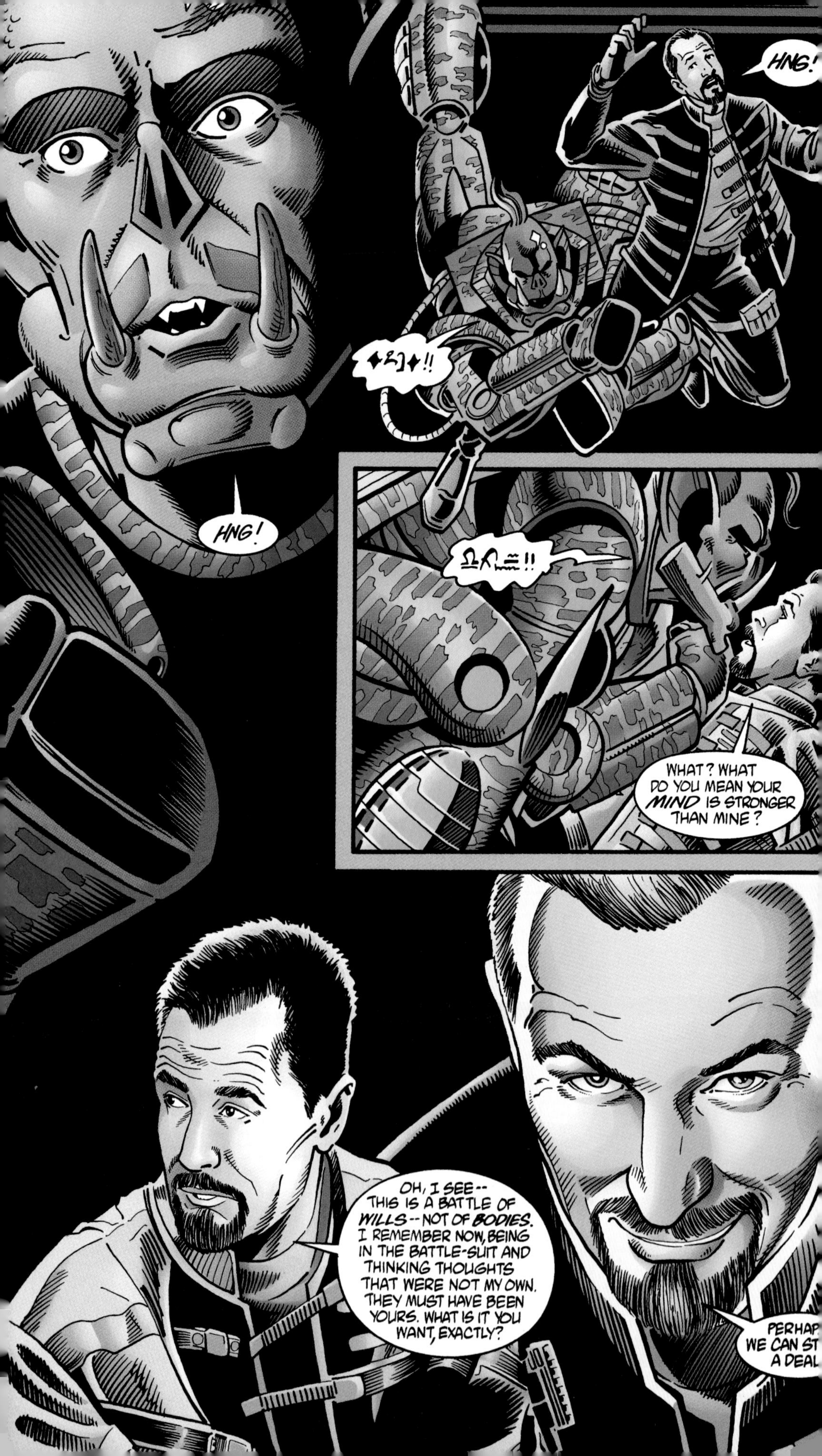
HNG!
HNG!
WHAT? WHAT DO YOU MEAN YOUR *MIND* IS STRONGER THAN MINE?
OH, I SEE -- THIS IS A BATTLE OF *WILLS* -- NOT OF *BODIES*. I REMEMBER NOW, BEING IN THE BATTLE-SUIT AND THINKING THOUGHTS THAT WERE NOT MY OWN. THEY MUST HAVE BEEN YOURS. WHAT IS IT YOU WANT, EXACTLY?
PERHAP WE CAN ST A DEAL

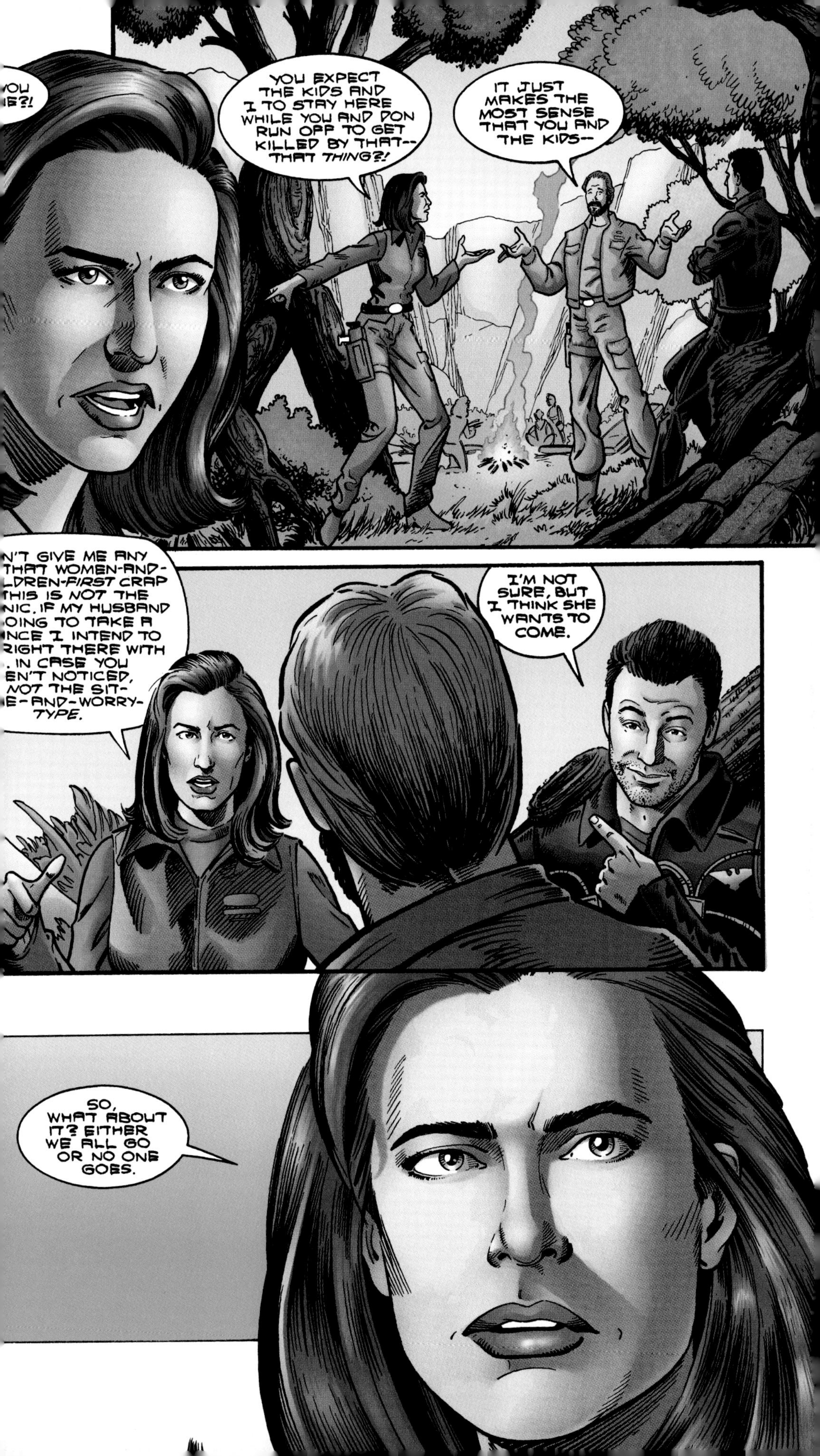

YOU E?!
YOU EXPECT THE KIDS AND I TO STAY HERE WHILE YOU AND DON RUN OFF TO GET KILLED BY THAT-- THAT *THING*?!
IT JUST MAKES THE MOST SENSE THAT YOU AND THE KIDS--
N'T GIVE ME ANY THAT WOMEN-AND-LDREN-*FIRST* CRAP THIS IS *NOT* THE NIC. IF MY HUSBAND OING TO TAKE A NCE I INTEND TO RIGHT THERE WITH . IN CASE YOU EN'T NOTICED, *NOT* THE SIT-E-AND-WORRY-*TYPE*.
I'M NOT SURE, BUT I THINK SHE WANTS TO COME.
SO, WHAT ABOUT IT? EITHER WE ALL GO OR NO ONE GOES.

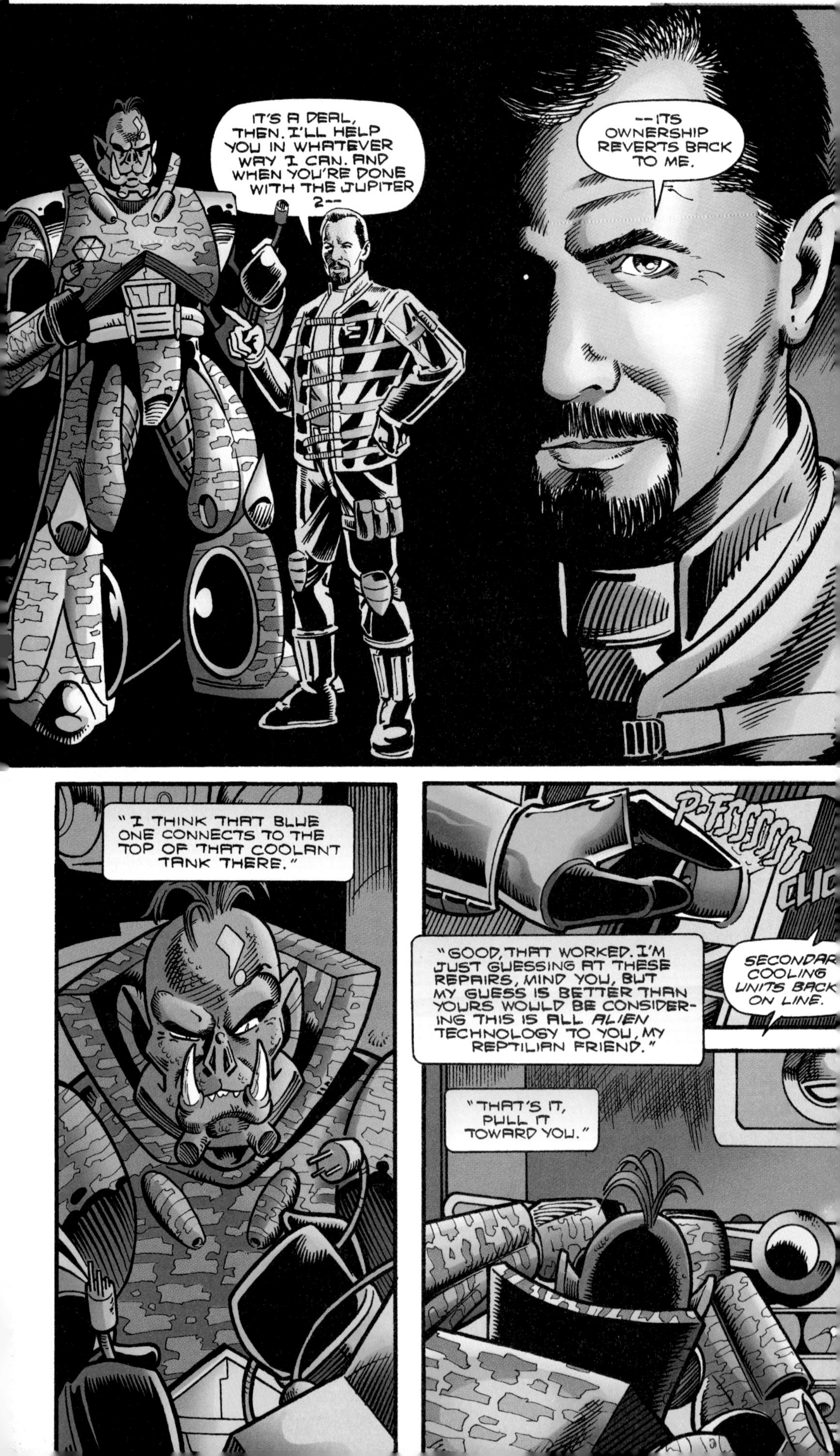

IT'S A DEAL, THEN. I'LL HELP YOU IN WHATEVER WAY I CAN. AND WHEN YOU'RE DONE WITH THE JUPITER 2--
--ITS OWNERSHIP REVERTS BACK TO ME.
"I THINK THAT BLUE ONE CONNECTS TO THE TOP OF THAT COOLANT TANK THERE."
P-TSSSSST
CLIC
"GOOD, THAT WORKED. I'M JUST GUESSING AT THESE REPAIRS, MIND YOU, BUT MY GUESS IS BETTER THAN YOURS WOULD BE CONSIDERING THIS IS ALL ALIEN TECHNOLOGY TO YOU, MY REPTILIAN FRIEND."
SECONDAR COOLING UNITS BACK ON LINE.
"THAT'S IT, PULL IT TOWARD YOU."

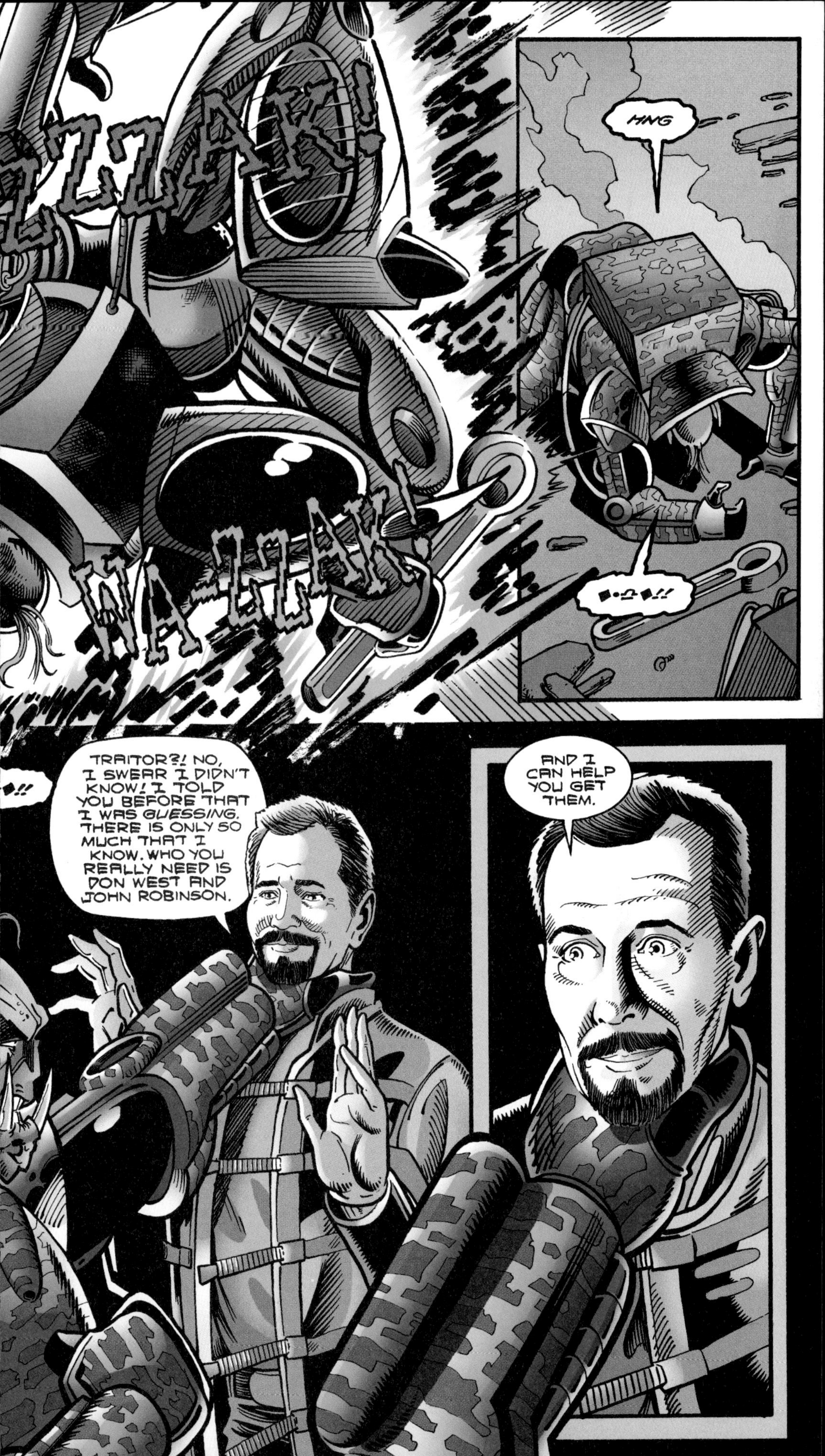
WA-ZZAK!
HNG
TRAITOR?! NO, I SWEAR I DIDN'T KNOW! I TOLD YOU BEFORE THAT I WAS *GUESSING*. THERE IS ONLY SO MUCH THAT I KNOW. WHO YOU REALLY NEED IS DON WEST AND JOHN ROBINSON.
AND I CAN HELP YOU GET THEM.

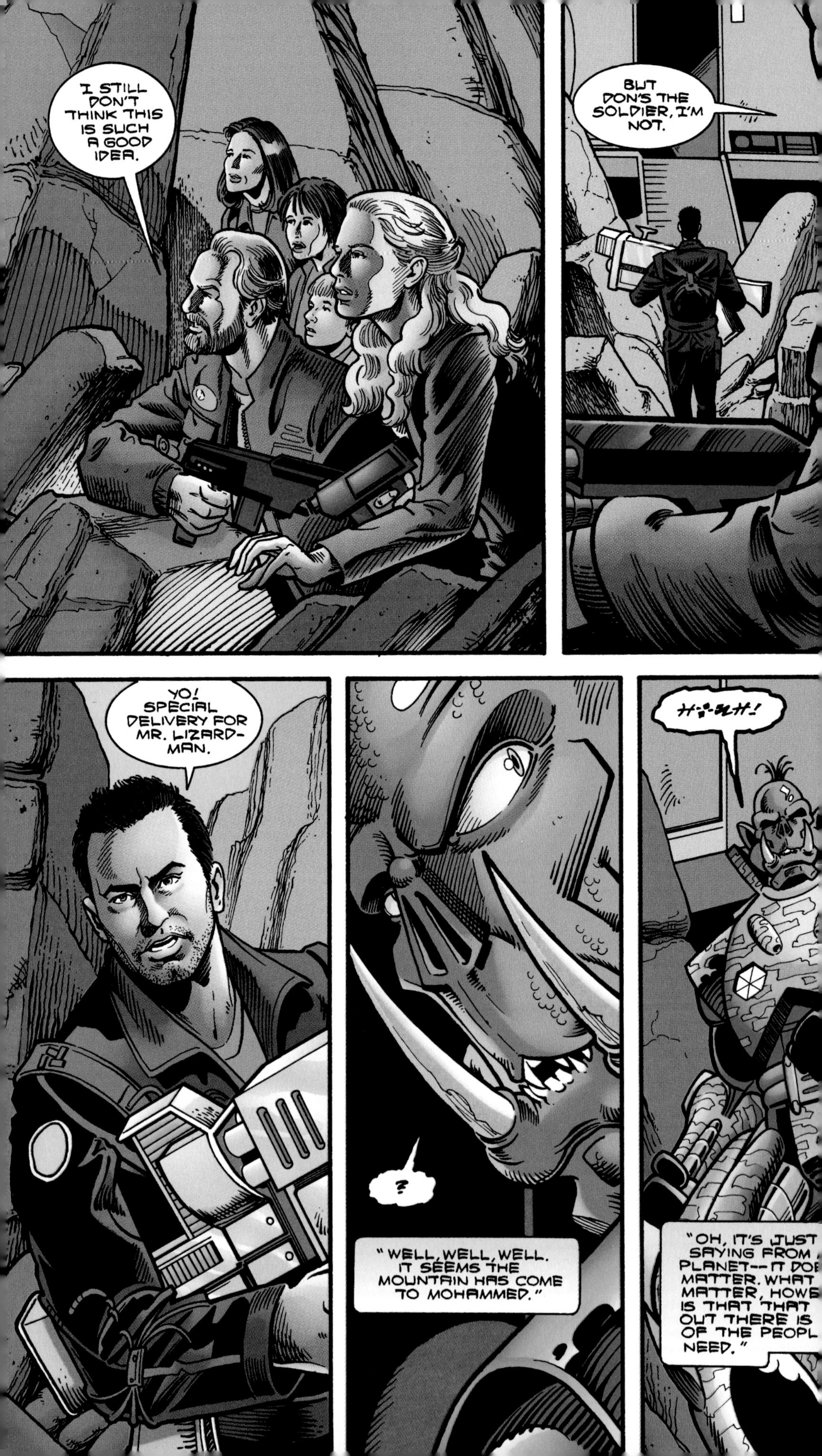

I STILL DON'T THINK THIS IS SUCH A GOOD IDEA.
BUT DON'S THE SOLDIER, I'M NOT.
YO! SPECIAL DELIVERY FOR MR. LIZARD-MAN.
?
"WELL, WELL, WELL. IT SEEMS THE MOUNTAIN HAS COME TO MOHAMMED."
"OH, IT'S JUST SAYING FROM PLANET-- IT DOE MATTER. WHAT MATTER, HOWE IS THAT THAT OUT THERE IS OF THE PEOPL NEED."

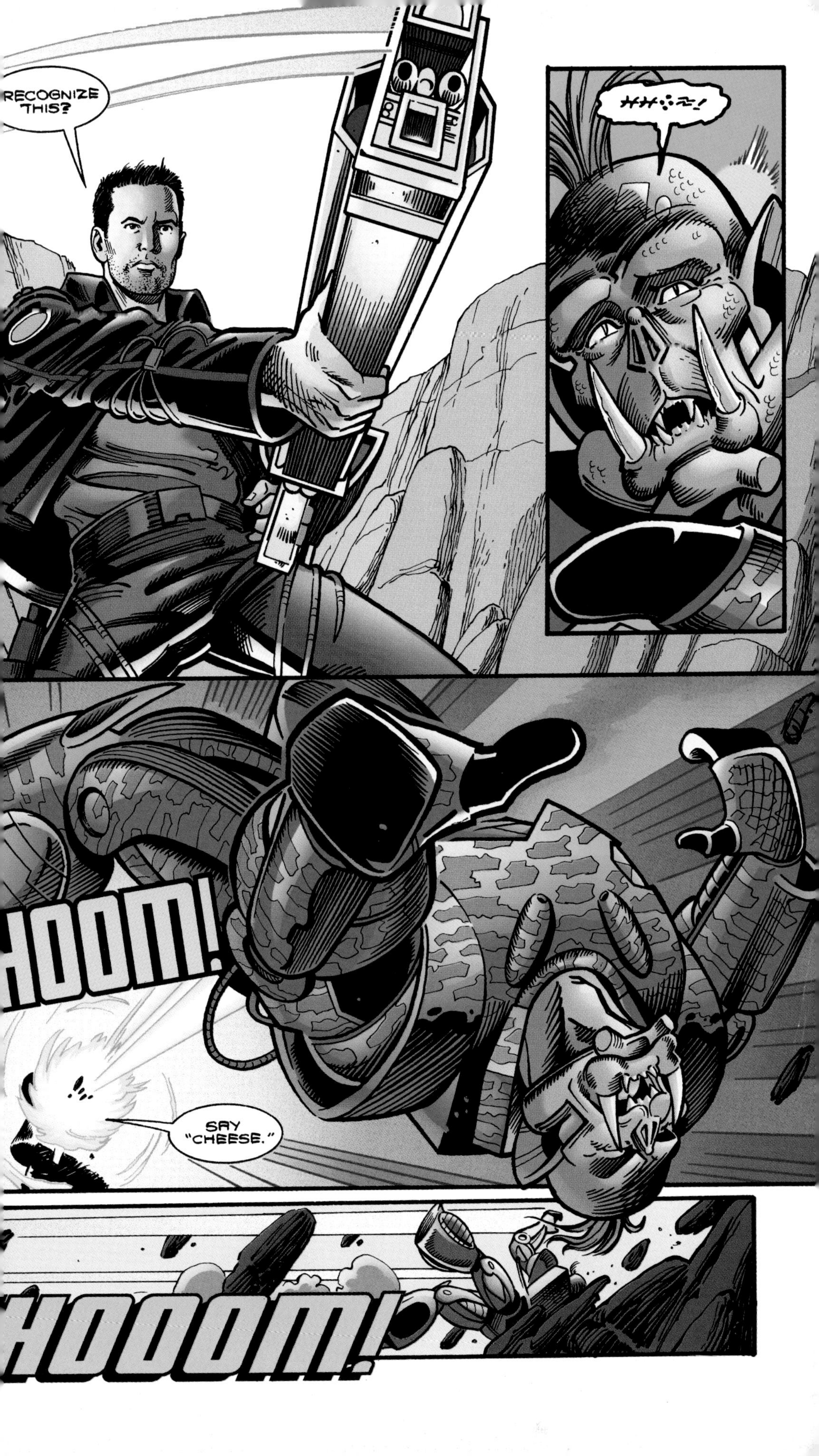
RECOGNIZE THIS?
HOOM!
SAY "CHEESE."
HOOOM!

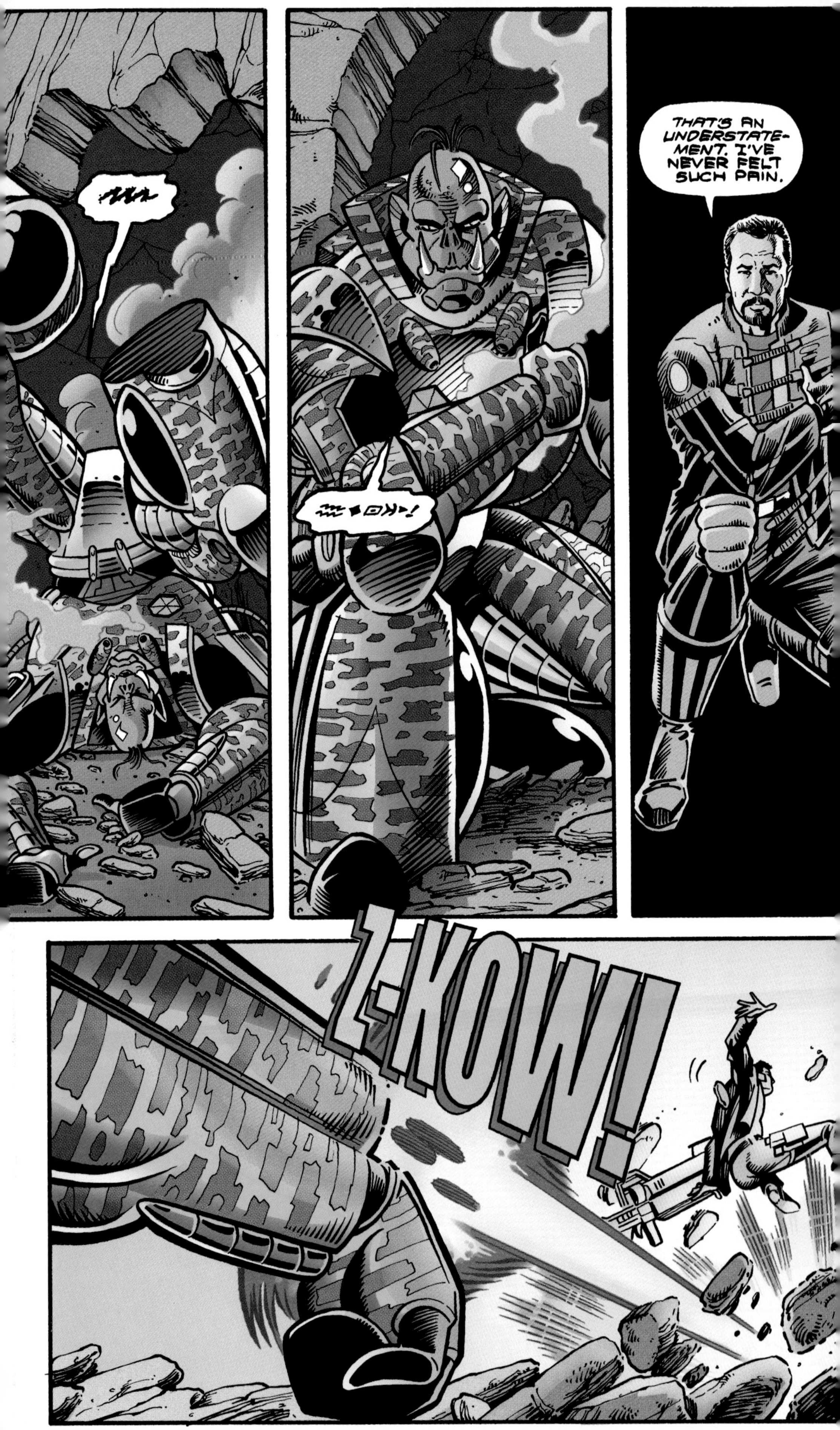
THAT'S AN UNDERSTATE-MENT. I'VE NEVER FELT SUCH PAIN.
Z-KOW!!

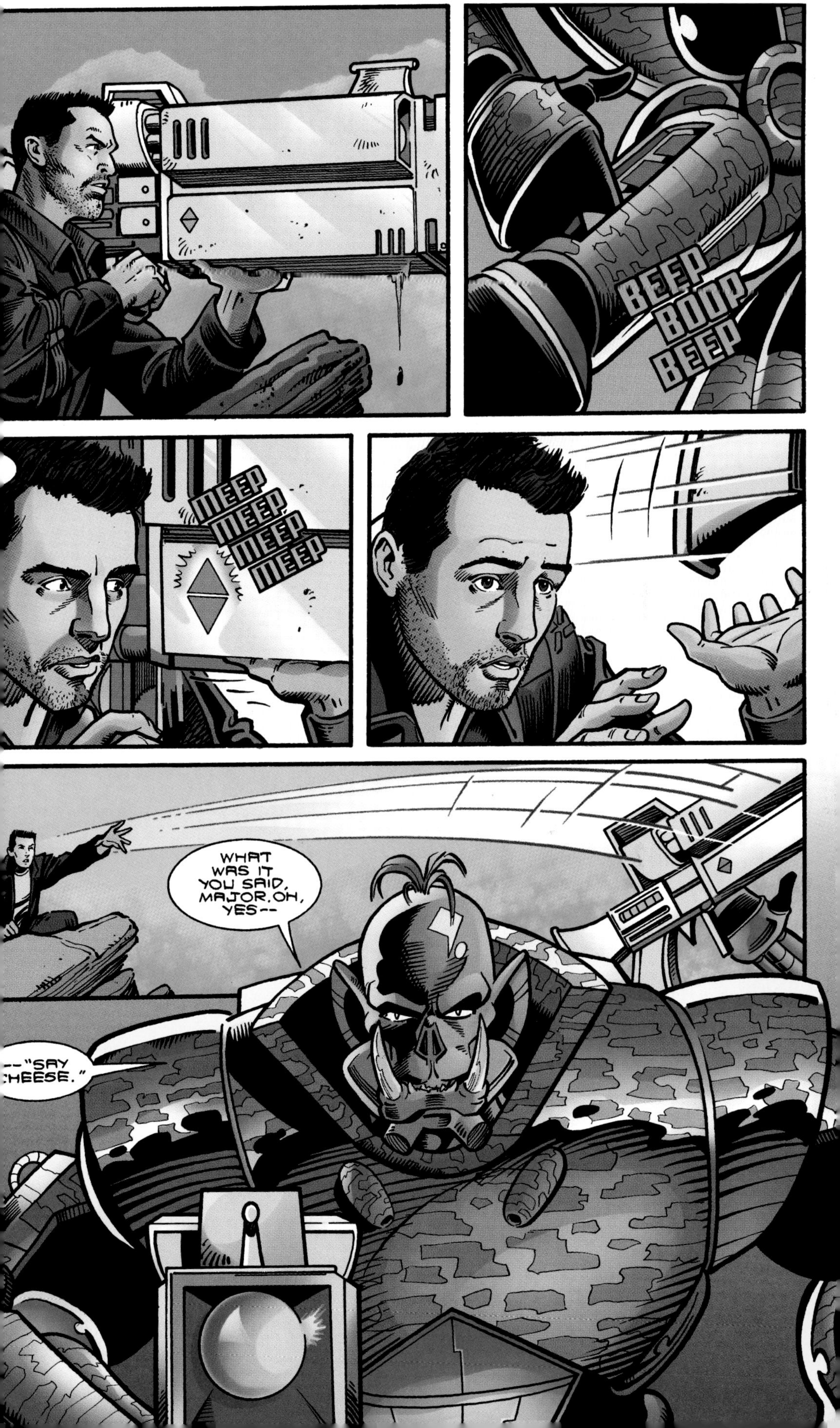
BEEP
BOOP
BEEP
MEEP
MEEP
MEEP
MEEP
WHAT WAS IT YOU SAID, MAJOR, OH, YES--
--"SAY CHEESE."

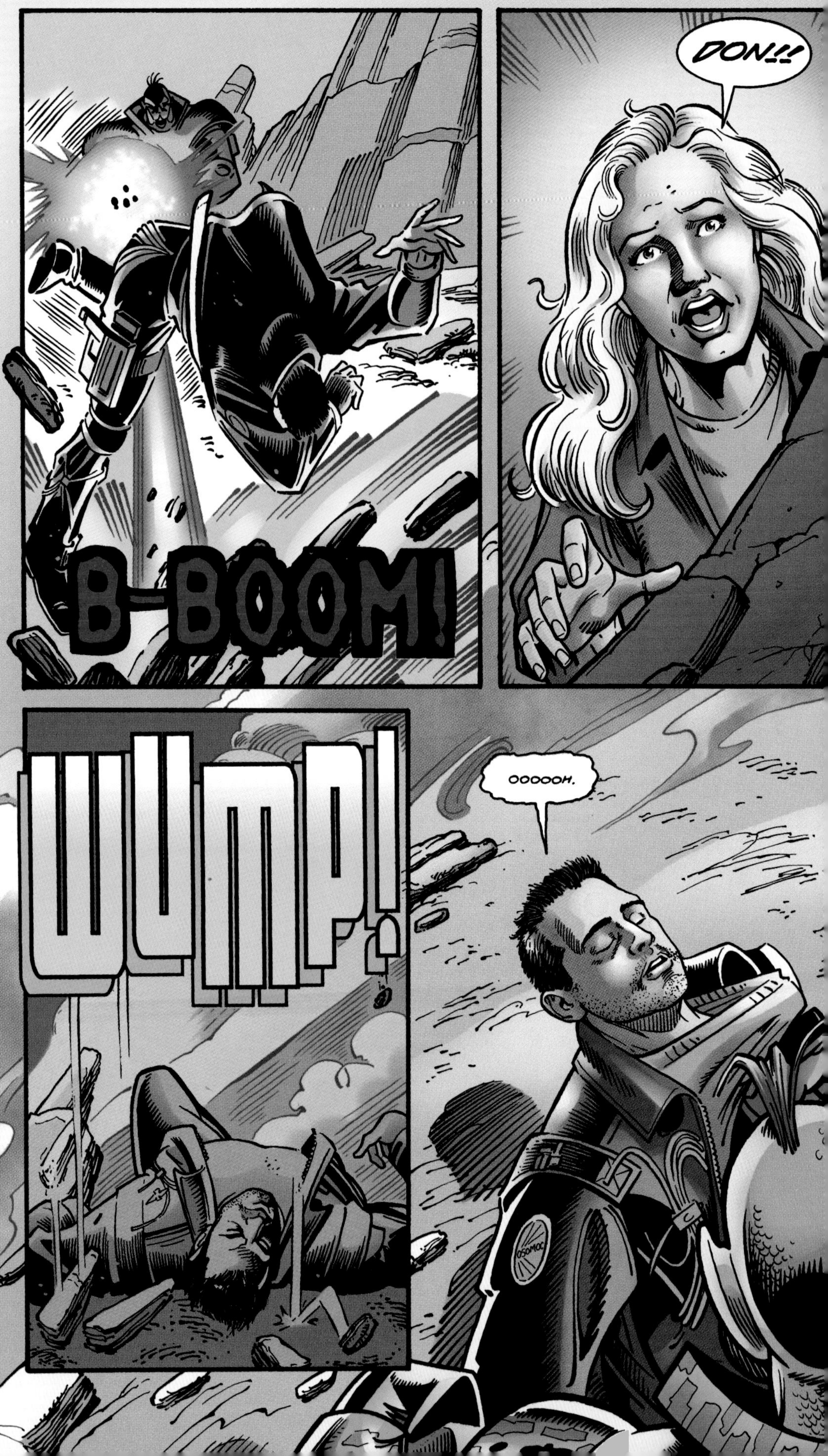
B-BOOM!
DON!!
WUMP!
OOOOOH.

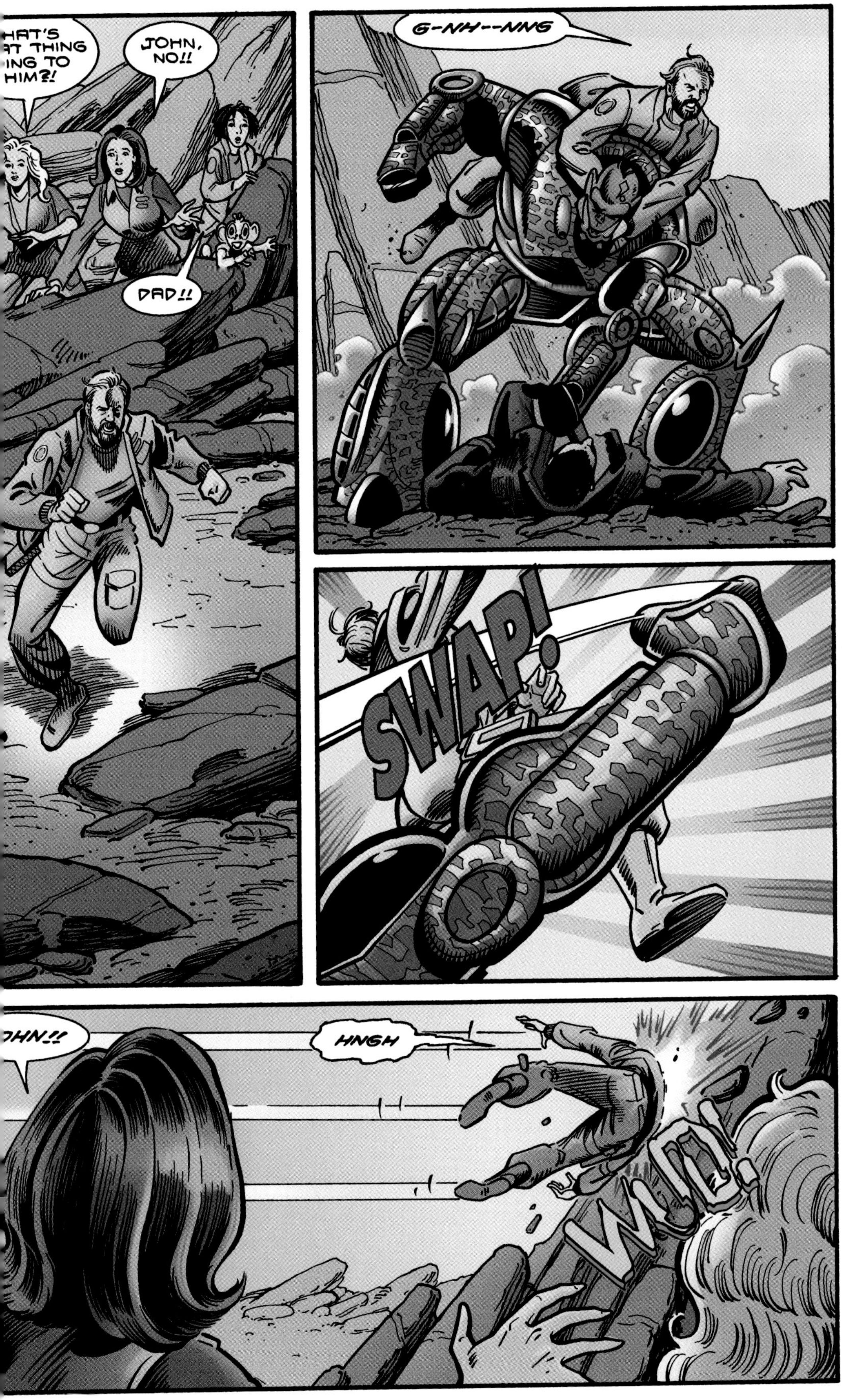
HAT'S
AT THING
ING TO
HIM?!
JOHN,
NO!!
DAD!!
G-NH--NNG
SWAP!
OHN!!
HNGH
WUD!

JOHN, CAN YOU HEAR ME? ARE YOU OKAY?

I'LL BE FINE--

--BUT WHAT'S THAT THING DOING TO DON?

DO NOT DIE, MAJOR WEST. IT IS NOT YET TIME.

SMITH...?

NO, NOT SMITH. HE HAS ALLOWED ME TO ACCESS HIS LANGUAGE CENTERS. I AM VOL-SCK.

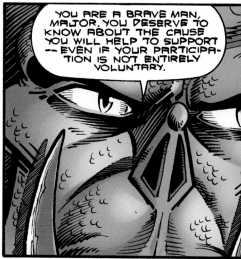

YOU ARE A BRAVE MAN, MAJOR. YOU DESERVE TO KNOW ABOUT THE CAUSE YOU WILL HELP TO SUPPORT -- EVEN IF YOUR PARTICIPATION IS NOT ENTIRELY VOLUNTARY.

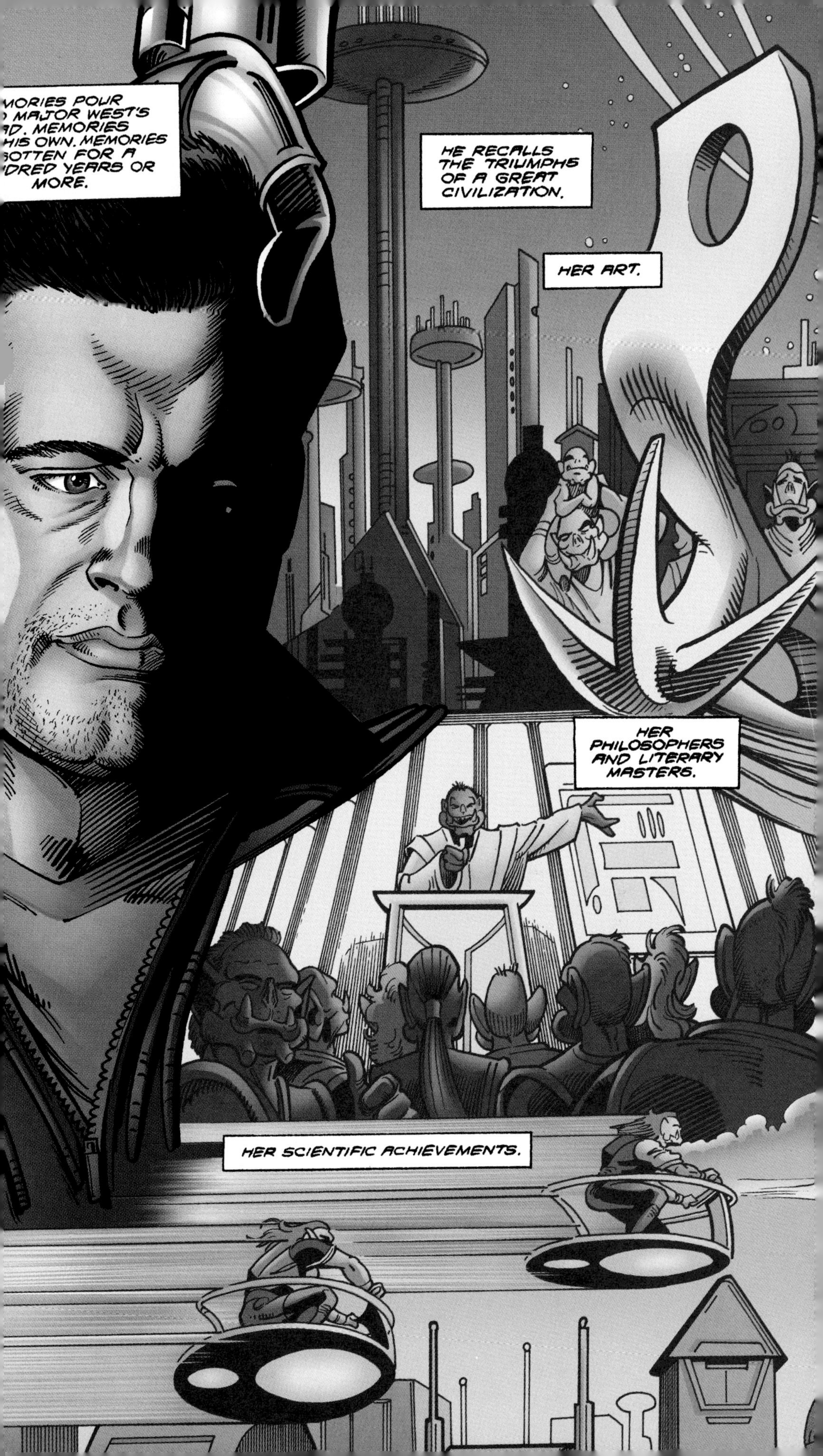
MORIES POUR
O MAJOR WEST'S
AD. MEMORIES
HIS OWN. MEMORIES
GOTTEN FOR A
NDRED YEARS OR
MORE.
HE RECALLS THE TRIUMPHS OF A GREAT CIVILIZATION.
HER ART.
HER PHILOSOPHERS AND LITERARY MASTERS.
HER SCIENTIFIC ACHIEVEMENTS.

AND THEN HE REMEMBERS THE WAR. THE WAR WITH A NEIGHBORING PLANET.

AND THEN A MEMORY NOT S FOREIGN TO D WEST. ONE OF ING A YOUNG SOLDIER WILL TO DIE OR KI FOR PRINCIP HE HOLDS D

HE REMEMBERS KNOWING THAT THE WAR WASN'T GOING WELL FOR HIS PEOPLE.

HE RECALLS THE PAIN OF BEING MORTALLY WOUNDED.

THERE WAS ONLY ONE CHANCE. HIS SCIENTISTS HAD DEVELOPED SOMETHING NEW. A WAY OF WINNING THE WAR FROM THE GRAVE.

ALTHOUGH HIS BO WAS DYING HE C PROGRAM HIS BR SUIT TO PRESER HIS ESSENCE. A AN ENEMY SHOU TRY TO CLAIM T SUIT AS A SPOIL WAR HE WOULD, SENSE, BE POSS BY THE SUITS VIOUS OWNER

TE TE T

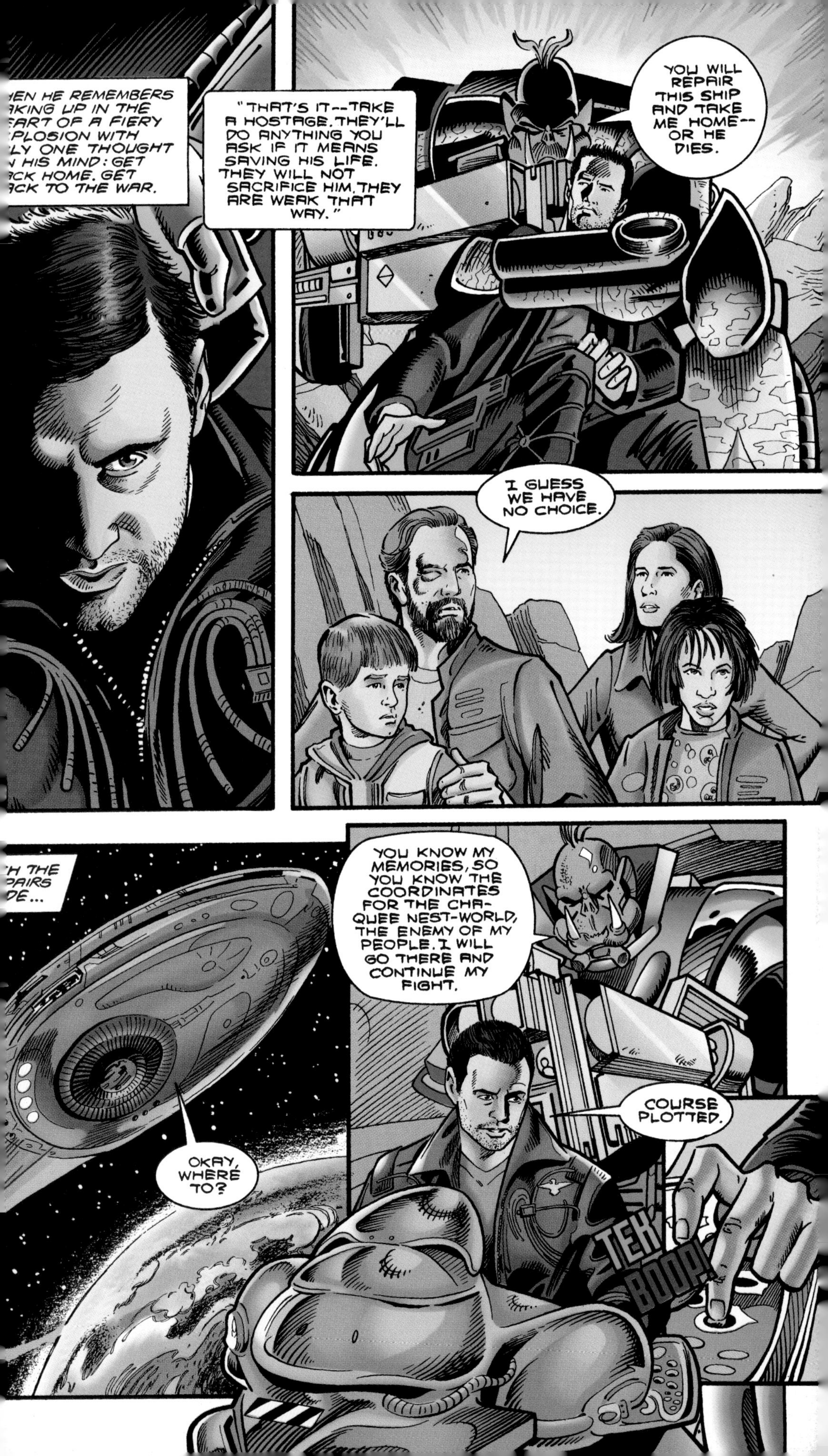

HEN HE REMEMBERS
AKING UP IN THE
EART OF A FIERY
PLOSION WITH
LY ONE THOUGHT
N HIS MIND: GET
CK HOME. GET
CK TO THE WAR.
"THAT'S IT--TAKE A HOSTAGE. THEY'LL DO ANYTHING YOU ASK IF IT MEANS SAVING HIS LIFE. THEY WILL NOT SACRIFICE HIM. THEY ARE WEAK THAT WAY."
YOU WILL REPAIR THIS SHIP AND TAKE ME HOME--OR HE DIES.
I GUESS WE HAVE NO CHOICE.
H THE
PAIRS
DE...
OKAY, WHERE TO?
YOU KNOW MY MEMORIES, SO YOU KNOW THE COORDINATES FOR THE CHA-QUEE NEST-WORLD, THE ENEMY OF MY PEOPLE. I WILL GO THERE AND CONTINUE MY FIGHT.
COURSE PLOTTED.
TEK
BOOP

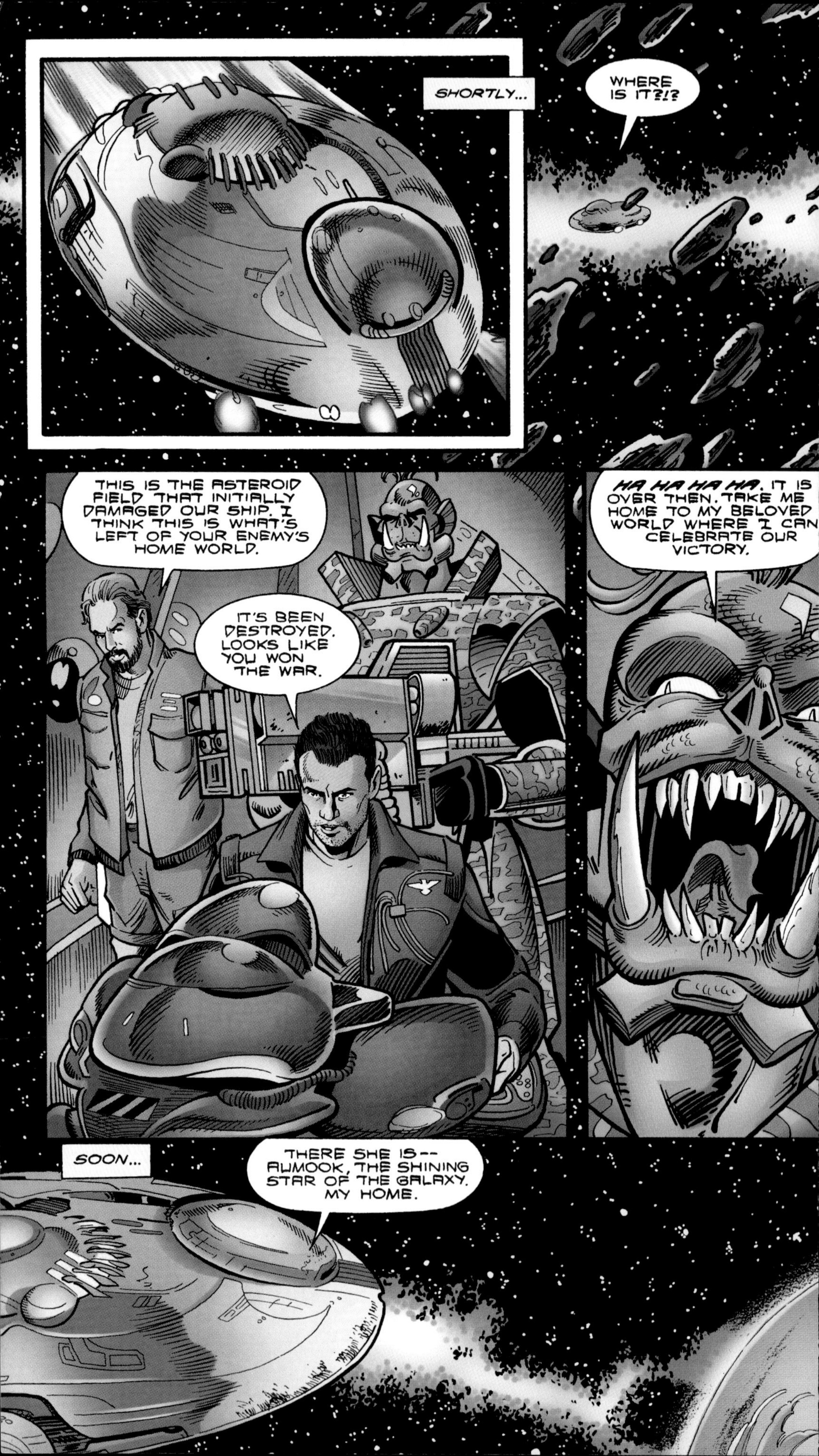
SHORTLY...
WHERE IS IT?!?
THIS IS THE ASTEROID FIELD THAT INITIALLY DAMAGED OUR SHIP. I THINK THIS IS WHAT'S LEFT OF YOUR ENEMY'S HOME WORLD.
IT'S BEEN DESTROYED. LOOKS LIKE YOU WON THE WAR.
HA HA HA HA. IT IS OVER THEN. TAKE ME HOME TO MY BELOVED WORLD WHERE I CAN CELEBRATE OUR VICTORY.
SOON...
THERE SHE IS -- AUMOOK, THE SHINING STAR OF THE GALAXY. MY HOME.

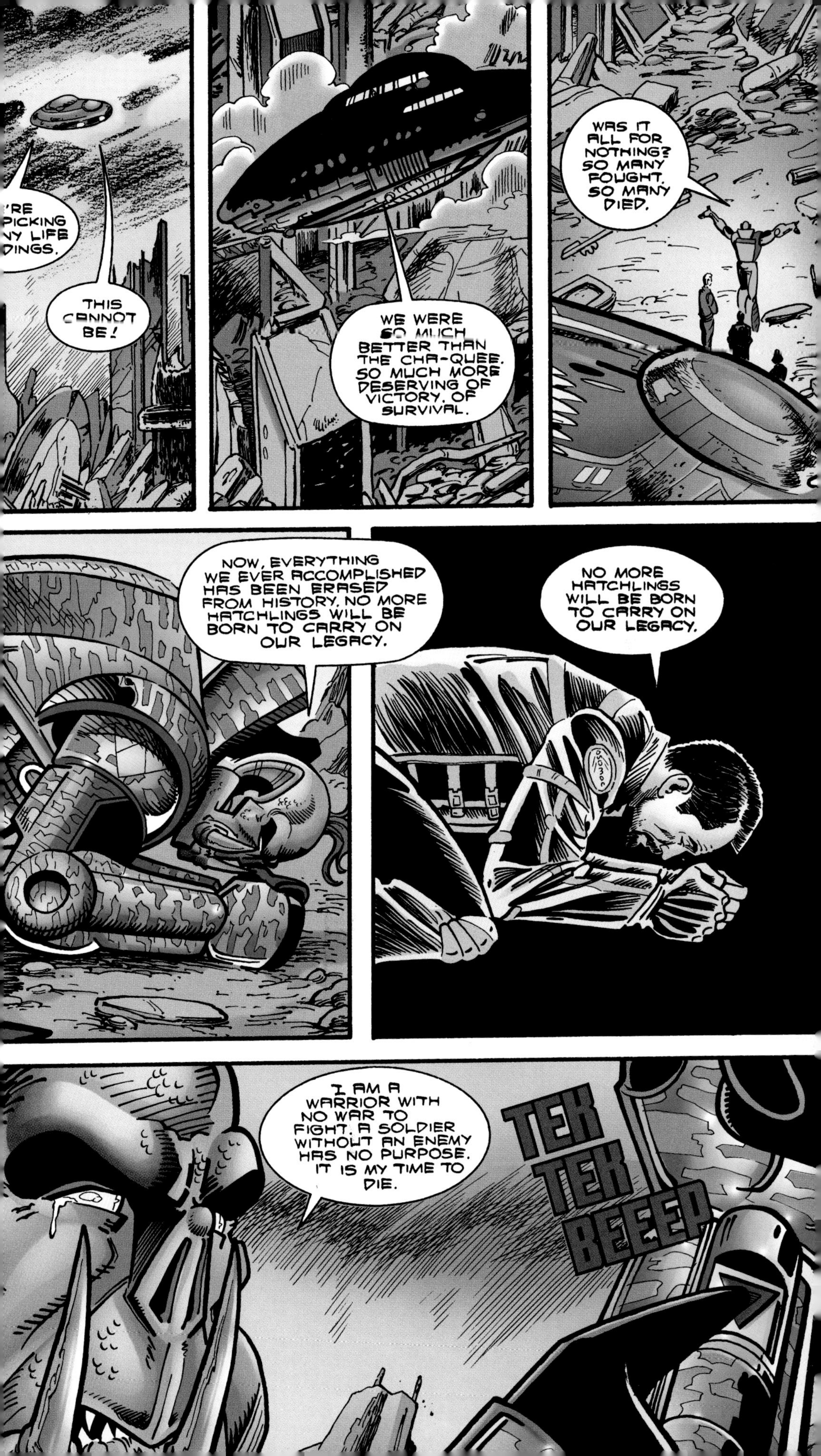
'RE PICKING NY LIFE DINGS.
THIS CANNOT BE!
WE WERE SO MUCH BETTER THAN THE CHA-QUEE. SO MUCH MORE DESERVING OF VICTORY, OF SURVIVAL.
WAS IT ALL FOR NOTHING? SO MANY FOUGHT, SO MANY DIED.
NOW, EVERYTHING WE EVER ACCOMPLISHED HAS BEEN ERASED FROM HISTORY. NO MORE HATCHLINGS WILL BE BORN TO CARRY ON OUR LEGACY.
NO MORE HATCHLINGS WILL BE BORN TO CARRY ON OUR LEGACY.
I AM A WARRIOR WITH NO WAR TO FIGHT. A SOLDIER WITHOUT AN ENEMY HAS NO PURPOSE. IT IS MY TIME TO DIE.
TEK TEK BEEEP

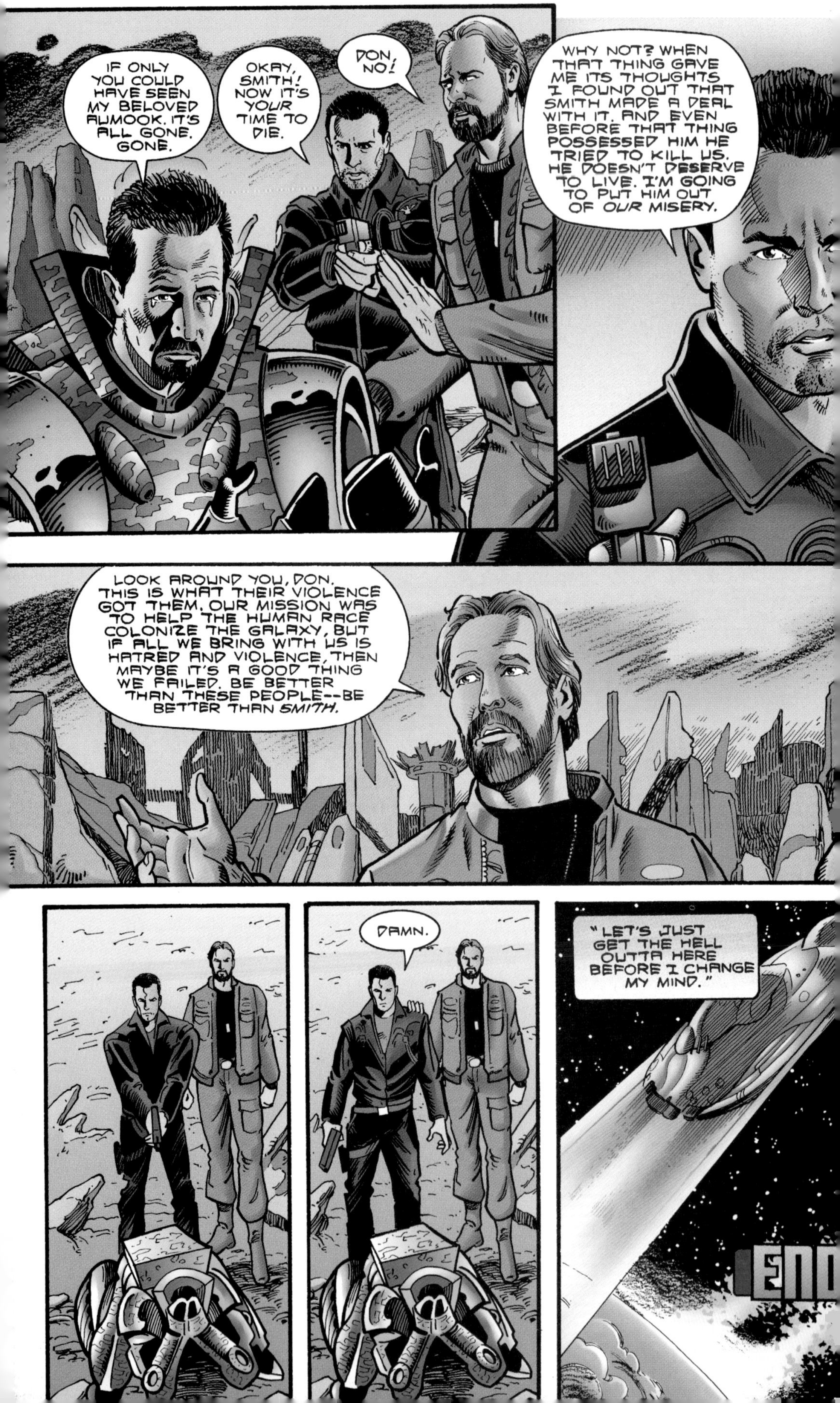

IF ONLY YOU COULD HAVE SEEN MY BELOVED AUMOOK. IT'S ALL GONE. GONE.
OKAY, SMITH! NOW IT'S YOUR TIME TO DIE.
DON, NO!
WHY NOT? WHEN THAT THING GAVE ME ITS THOUGHTS I FOUND OUT THAT SMITH MADE A DEAL WITH IT. AND EVEN BEFORE THAT THING POSSESSED HIM HE TRIED TO KILL US. HE DOESN'T DESERVE TO LIVE. I'M GOING TO PUT HIM OUT OF OUR MISERY.
LOOK AROUND YOU, DON. THIS IS WHAT THEIR VIOLENCE GOT THEM. OUR MISSION WAS TO HELP THE HUMAN RACE COLONIZE THE GALAXY, BUT IF ALL WE BRING WITH US IS HATRED AND VIOLENCE, THEN MAYBE IT'S A GOOD THING WE FAILED. BE BETTER THAN THESE PEOPLE--BE BETTER THAN SMITH.
DAMN.
"LET'S JUST GET THE HELL OUTTA HERE BEFORE I CHANGE MY MIND."

FOLLOWING ARE THE COVERS FROM
DARK HORSE COMICS' **LOST IN SPACE**
ISSUES #2 & #3, BY

GARY ERSKINE &
GORDON PURCELL

COLORED AND SEPARATED BY

DARK HORSE DIGITAL

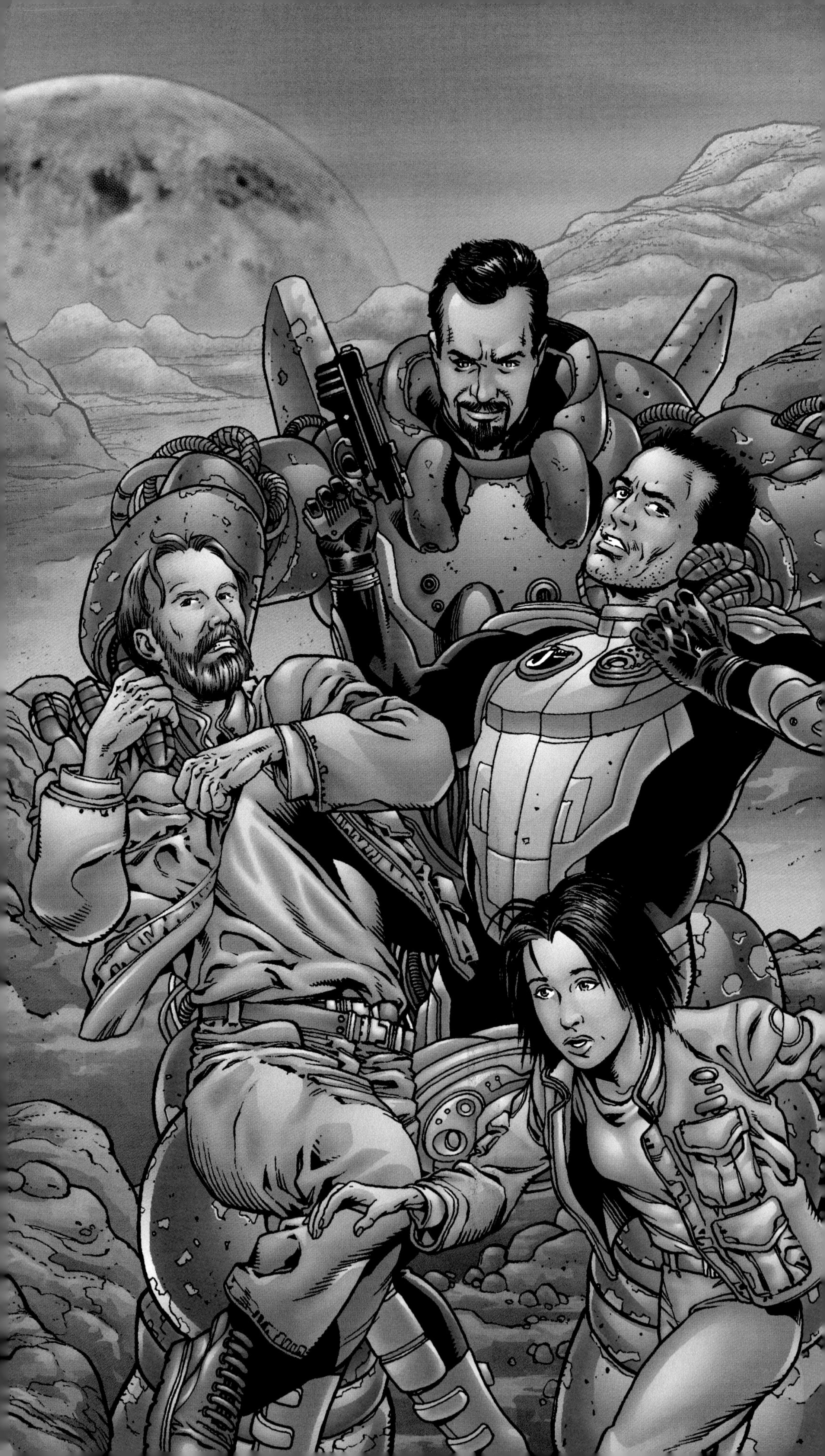

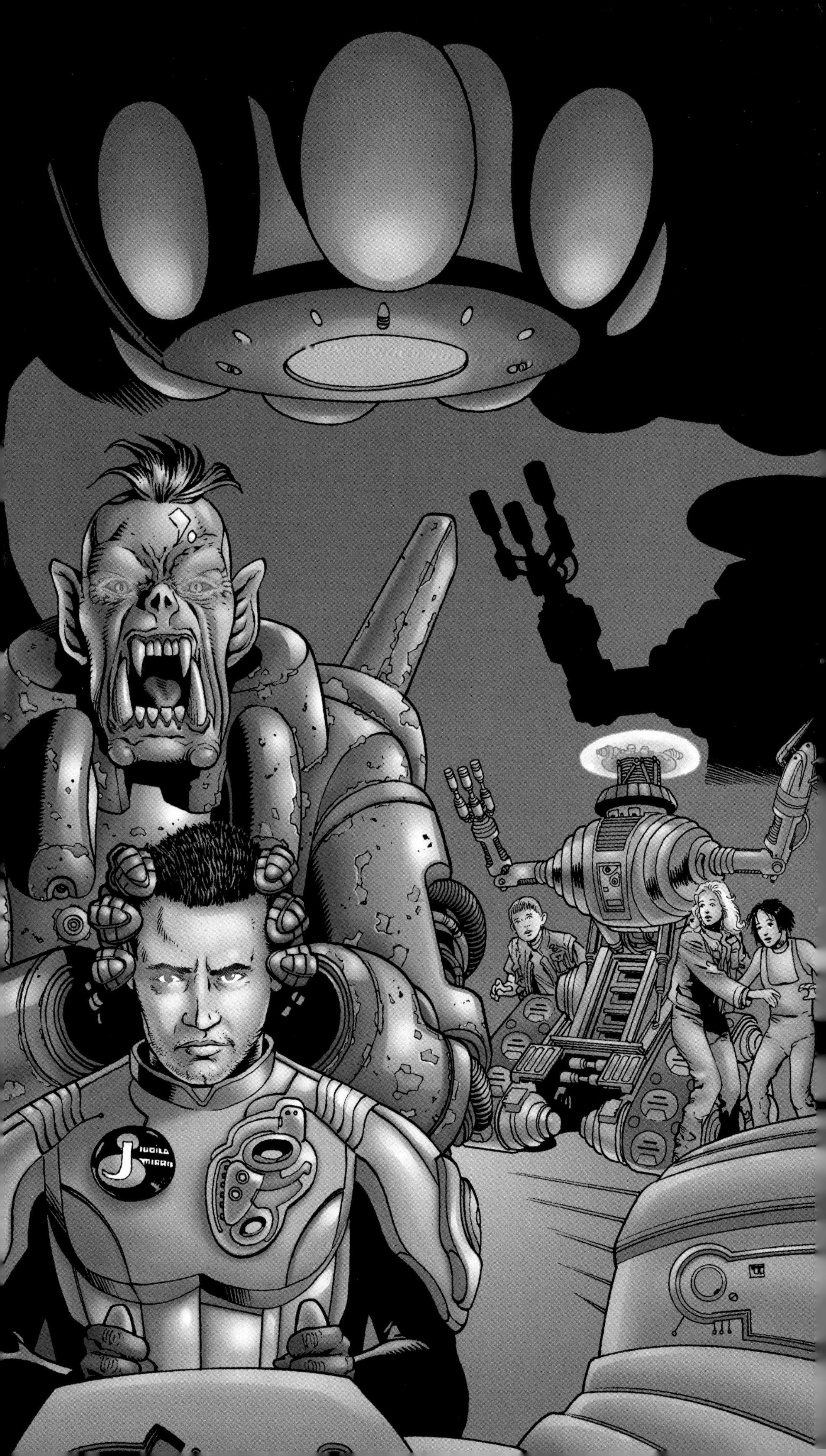